Ellie,
ENGINEER
The Next Level

Books by Jackson Pearce

The Doublecross

The Inside Job

Ellie, Engineer

Ellie, Engineer: The Next Level

Ellie, Engineer: In the Spotlight

Praise for Jackson Pearce

"Offers an important message about how making assumptions and believing stereotypes can hurt people." –*School Library Connection*

"A structurally sound story about challenging assumptions and responsible engineering." –*Kirkus Reviews*

"A solid STEM-themed book with a strong focus on empowering young women to embrace and pursue their interests." –*School Library Journal*

Ellie, ENGINEER

"A charming book featuring an engineer who makes mistakes when navigating the roads of friendship." –*School Library Journal*

"Explicitly rejects the idea that activities and objects are gendered (e.g., boys and girls can both like engineering and tea parties). . . . A spirited, duplicable depiction of STEM fun." –*Kirkus Reviews*

"The engaging storyline allows the reader to visualize how Ellie thinks in terms of STEM concepts while she's inventing, making this a perfect read aloud for STEM enthusiasts." –*School Library Connection*

"Ellie's easily relatable as an everyday kid. . . . Aspiring inventors will appreciate the descriptions and black and white sketches of Ellie's various creations." –*BCCB*

THE DOUBLECROSS

"Fast-paced, funny, and full of unexpected plot twists, this spy novel will easily appeal to middle grade adventure fans." –*School Library Journal*

"A zany, fun adventure, with Hale a kind and clever protagonist. Oddball characters with plenty of heart and nifty gadgets will draw in readers who appreciate humorous underdog stories." –*Booklist*

"Exciting missions, cool gadgets, and plenty of intrigue make this a fun read from the get-go. . . . International espionage plus wacky high jinks equals plot-twisting fun." –*Kirkus Reviews*

"An entertaining and memorable story." –*Publishers Weekly*

THE INSIDE JOB

"A fun-filled adventure from start to finish." –*Booklist*

"A funny, smart spy adventure with strong characters and clever twists." –*School Library Journal*

"This sequel will continue to thrill fans of the series. Wacky and action-packed." –*Kirkus Reviews*

JACKSON PEARCE

ILLUSTRATED BY

TUESDAY MOURNING

BLOOMSBURY
CHILDREN'S BOOKS
NEW YORK LONDON OXFORD NEW DELHI SYDNEY

BLOOMSBURY CHILDREN'S BOOKS
Bloomsbury Publishing Inc., part of Bloomsbury Publishing Plc
1385 Broadway, New York, NY 10018

BLOOMSBURY, BLOOMSBURY CHILDREN'S BOOKS, and the Diana logo are trademarks of Bloomsbury Publishing Plc

First published in the United States of America in November 2018
by Bloomsbury Children's Books
Paperback edition published in November 2019

ISBN 978-1-5476-0206-3 (paperback)

The Library of Congress has cataloged the hardcover edition as follows:
Names: Pearce, Jackson, author.
Title: Ellie, engineer : the next level / by Jackson Pearce.
Description: New York : Bloomsbury, 2018.
Summary: When Ellie and her friends help elderly Mrs. Curran around the house, Ellie cannot resist using her engineering process, but it is no fun for the girls when Toby gets the credit.
Identifiers: LCCN 2017056222
ISBN 978-1-68119-521-6 (hardcover) • ISBN 978-1-68119-522-3 (e-book)
Subjects: | CYAC: Engineering–Fiction. | Building–Fiction. | Sex role–Fiction. | Friendship–Fiction. | Neighborliness–Fiction.
Classification: LCC PZ7.P31482 Elt 2018 (print) | DCC [Fic]–dc23
LC record available at https://lccn.loc.gov/2017056222

Book design by Jeanette Levy
Typeset by Westchester Publishing Services
Printed and bound in the U.S.A. by Berryville Graphics Inc., Berryville, Virginia
2 4 6 8 10 9 7 5 3 1

For my mom,
who never said "girls can't"

Chapter One

Ellie Bell was building something new.

This wasn't weird or anything, because Ellie was basically *always* building something new. It was pretty much her favorite thing to do, especially during the summer: come up with a new project, design it, then build it with her friends Kit and Toby.

What *was* weird about this particular

something new was the fact that it involved twenty-four jars of bread-and-butter pickles.

"Does it still look flat to you?" Ellie called out to Toby. Toby was in Ellie's playhouse, which doubled as her workshop—it was full of tools and bits of wood and loose screws she'd collected in peanut butter jars. Right now, Toby was staring out the playhouse window, narrowing his eyes at the scuffed-up tabletop they'd found in someone's trash a few days ago. Kit didn't like it so much when Ellie got excited about something from the trash—Kit was a very tidy person—but Ellie knew sometimes people threw away really, really useful stuff.

The tabletop had two ropes—one on each end—that were knotted together in the middle. Right now, it was hovering just an inch or so off the ground, so Ellie could make sure it stayed nice and flat in the air.

"It looks flat to me," Toby called back down,

putting his hands around his mouth to make his voice louder.

"What about from there?" Ellie asked Kit, who was standing on the porch, looking at the tabletop through pink binoculars, even though she wasn't really that far away from the workshop. Kit was wearing a T-shirt that had a dog wearing heart-shaped sunglasses on it. Ellie was wearing the same one—they'd decided the T-shirts were lucky, since whenever they were wearing them, they built something really good, or the ice-cream truck came around the neighborhood, or they wrote a really funny joke together.

"We're go for flat!" Kit answered, waving a thumbs-up in the air.

"Great!" Ellie said. She climbed the ladder up to her workshop and nudged Toby over a little bit. Right by the door, there was a chain from Toby's old swing set. It went out the playhouse door and to a piece of the workshop roof, where Ellie had it looped around a back wheel from her old tricycle—one without the tire—then down to the tabletop. The tricycle wheel with the rope made a pulley! Pulleys were machines, just very simple ones—but that didn't make them any less cool, because they made it way easier to lift super-heavy things up into the air.

"Most elevators don't use swing-set chains," Toby said, shaking his head. That's what this build was—an elevator for the workshop. Once it was done, Ellie wouldn't need to make a billion trips up and down the ladder to take things into her workshop. *And* it would be a way for people who couldn't climb the ladder, like her grandma or Lacey from school (who had a glittery pink wheelchair), to get up into the workshop if they wanted to come visit.

"Well, most elevators are for much taller buildings," Ellie pointed out. "And they *do* use pulleys, like we're using. Just lots of really giant pulleys instead of one made out of a tricycle wheel."

Toby nodded, looking thoughtful. "That's true. I looked it up last night, and most elevators have to be inspected. Do you have an inspector coming? You can schedule an inspector on weekdays, according to the website I saw."

Toby got like this now and then. People in class sometimes called him a know-it-all—Ellie, in fact, used to call him that a lot. She didn't really anymore, though, because now she knew that Toby was just *Toby*, just like she was just Ellie and Kit was just Kit. It didn't seem right to be friends with Toby but still call him a name behind his back, even if he did still make her sigh a little here and there.

"Maybe *you* can be the inspector," Ellie suggested, taking hold of the chain.

"I do know a lot about elevators, now," Toby said, looking pleased. He folded his arms and pulled in his eyebrows, and Ellie had to admit, he did look very inspector-y.

"Perfect!" Ellie said, then looked out the workshop door to Kit, who was watching birds through her binoculars. "Keep an eye on it, Kit!" Ellie yelled. "Ready? One, two, *three*!"

On three, she pulled back on the chain. It slid through the tricycle-wheel-pulley and tightened all the way down to the tabletop. She pulled some more, and the tabletop began to rise off the ground, inching up toward the workshop. When it was level with the floor, Ellie stopped, then wrapped the chain around a high-heeled shoe she'd nailed to the floor (it made a handy doorstop and didn't hurt your toes when you stepped on it barefoot).

"Woohoo!" Kit cheered from below.

"Inspection part one, passed!" Toby said, and high-fived Ellie. She grinned. Building projects were always better when Toby and Kit were with her.

"Are we ready for these?" Kit asked, nudging a thick-sided cardboard box with her toe. It was stacked two rows high with glass jars of pickles that said *In a Pickle* in swirly writing on the side. They'd found the box and the pickles in Kit's garage, and Ellie had done a little math: Each jar of pickles weighed two and a half pounds. She, Kit, and Toby all weighed about sixty pounds each. So, if the elevator was strong enough to lift twenty-four jars of pickles—which was every single jar—it could definitely lift a person. Ellie thought it was pretty lucky how quickly they'd found something to test the elevator with. Sometimes engineering just worked out like that!

"Sure, let's do it!" Ellie answered Kit's

question. Really, she knew they ought to test the elevator with one jar of pickles at a time, just to be safe . . . but the first test had gone so well! Besides, the sooner they proved *all* the pickles could be lifted, the sooner they could start riding up and down on the elevator themselves.

Ellie and Toby hurried down the workshop ladder. The three of them began to haul the jars of pickles out of the box and onto the tabletop—onto the *elevator*—stacking them up neatly. Toby even made sure all the labels were facing the same way, like they do at the grocery store. When they were done, and the summer sunshine was hitting the pickles just right, it looked like the jars were filled with magical green potion.

Well, pickles in magical green potion, anyway.

Ellie checked the knots, then pulled her hammer from her tool belt and tap-tap-tapped on the nails holding the tabletop together, just to double-check they were all good. Yep—all the knots were so tight, they were like little rocks made of rope.

It was elevator time.

The three of them scrambled back up the workshop ladder, Kit and Toby poking their heads out the windows on either side of the door so they could get a good view of the build in action. Ellie took a deep breath—the excited kind, with just a little bit of the nervous kind way in the back of her throat—and grabbed hold of the chain.

"*Oof*," she said, pulling back.

Pickles were really heavy when there were twenty-four jars of them stacked together. The elevator had barely moved an inch off the ground.

"*Ooooooof*," Ellie said, pulling back even harder.

"I thought the pulley was supposed to make it easy to lift," Kit said, frowning. "Here, let me try."

Kit was pretty strong, so Ellie handed over the chain. She pulled with her whole body, but the elevator hardly moved. Toby didn't have any luck either.

"Maybe we ought to try together?" Kit said thoughtfully, and took the chain from Toby's hands. Kit, Toby, and Ellie all grabbed hold of a different section of the chain. Ellie took a breath and gripped it so tightly that it pinched her fingers.

"One, two, *pull!*" she said, and together, they hauled back on the chain. The tabletop lifted! The elevator was working!

For a second, anyway.

Then things went . . . well, *sideways.* Literally.

The tabletop suddenly tilted just a teeny

bit, but that was all it took—because before Ellie or her friends could react, the pickle jars began to *slide* down the tabletop. Ellie yelped, Kit squealed, and Toby said, "Oh, no, no, no, no, no" so fast it sounded more like he was humming than speaking.

Twenty-four pickle jars slid off the end of the tabletop. They crashed to the ground, but Ellie didn't see it happen, because as soon as they fell, the rope became light, and she and her friends tumbled backward into a heap of elbows and knees.

"This isn't good," Ellie said, rubbing the spot where she'd smacked her head on Kit's kneecap.

"Pickle juice is sometimes called *brine.* It's very acidic. It might kill the grass," Toby answered.

"Do you think they all broke? Do you think my mom will notice?" Kit said worriedly, sticking out her hands to help Ellie and Toby up. Her fingernails still had baby chicks painted on them from when she and Ellie had played nail salon the day before. Okay, they mostly looked like yellow blobs, but they were *supposed* to be chicks. Ellie just didn't understand how the people on the videos they'd watched were so good at painting pictures on such a tiny little nail.

They winced and hobbled over to the edge of the workshop and looked down.

Twenty-four jars of pickles, all cracked open, pickles strewn across the grass. The tabletop was flipped over, the ropes were tossed around like spaghetti noodles, and the pickle juice smell was extra strong and sting-y sweet in the summer air. It didn't look like a single jar of In a Pickle pickles had survived the fall.

"Maybe we should have started with pillows instead of glass jars?" Ellie suggested a little weakly, and pulled out her notebook, flipping to the page where she'd sketched out the elevator. "Or maybe if we . . . hmm . . . I wonder if there's a way to keep the stuff on the elevator from wobbling–"

"Um, Ellie? I think before we fix this build, we'd better fix . . . well . . . *this*," Kit said, motioning to the pile of pickles with one hand and biting the nails of the other.

"I don't think we can fix this," Toby said, shaking his head.

"Well, at least clean it up?" Kit replied.

"You can't really clean it up. The brine is soaked into the dirt now. The grass is doomed."

Ellie wanted to glare at Toby because he was totally not helping, but the truth was, she felt like a lot more than the grass was doomed– especially once Kit's mom found out. She thought about the back of her notepad, where she always wrote down projects once they were finished and working and great.

She definitely would *not* be adding Project 63: Workshop Elevator to that list today.

Chapter Two

It was bad enough that they'd broken twenty-four jars of pickles, which it turned out Kit's mom had bought to dice up and put in egg salad sandwiches for a fancy luncheon. Ellie didn't really understand the difference between a *luncheon* and just regular *lunch*, but she knew this was not the time to ask. To make matters worse, however, it turned out that pickle juice attracts gnats, flies, mosquitos, wasps, and yellow jackets. Ellie's dad was outside cleaning up all the broken glass, wearing long sleeves to keep from being bitten or stung, even though it was about a billion degrees.

Ellie was sitting on the kitchen barstool, hoping that if she stayed very, very still, her dad wouldn't even notice her when he came back inside. Her mom was over at Kit's house, trying to help Kit's mother find replacement pickles. ("You can't just *replace* In a Pickle pickles! They're special order!" Kit's mom had wailed.) Ellie felt badly but still thought it seemed very strange to special-order pickles—though that was exactly the sort of thing Kit's mom would do.

Outside, Ellie heard the jingle of the ice-cream truck's bell. She sighed and looked down at her lucky dog-in-sunglasses T-shirt. She wished the luck could have gone toward the project today, instead of the ice-cream truck's showing up. She couldn't stop herself from wondering, though, what went so wrong with the elevator. Maybe she should have put more ropes on the platform? Oh, or maybe the platform needed to be bigger! Or—

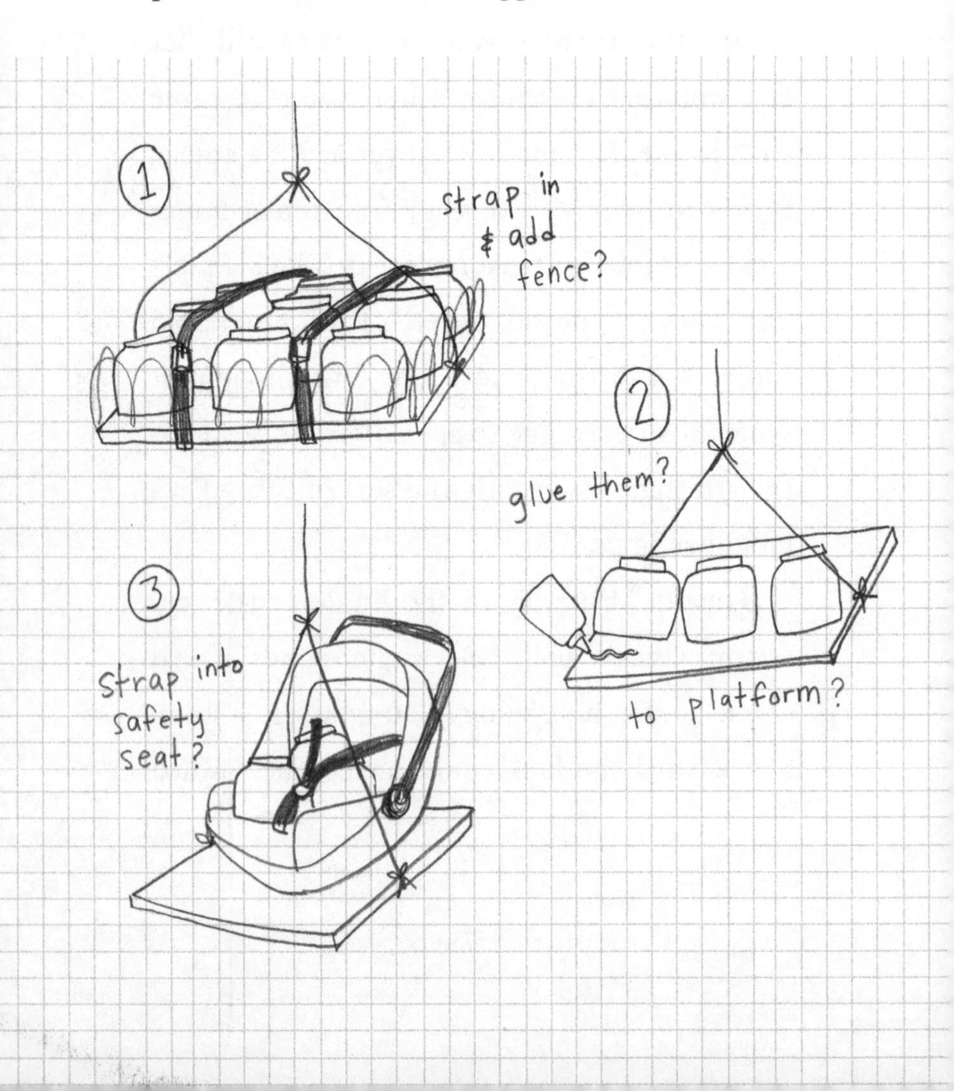

"Well," Ellie's dad said, interrupting her thoughts when he walked back inside. There were some gnats stuck to the pickle-juice-sweat on his head. He took a big breath of the air-conditioned air, then shut the door behind him. "Ellie, what should we do about this?"

Ellie rubbed the back of her neck. "It seemed so stable! I didn't *mean* for it to crash," she said. "What did I do wrong in the build?"

Ellie's dad frowned. "Well, you probably didn't account for the sloshing–wait, no, this isn't about the build!" Ellie's dad said, cutting himself off. He went on, "It's not about the build–it's about the fact that you took something that belonged to Kit's mother without permission and broke it. And apparently those are some very fancy pickles," he said, and shook his head–he seemed to think it was as strange to special-order pickles as Ellie did.

"We didn't *know* they would break. We just

wanted something that weighed about the same as a person. It didn't seem smart to use an *actual* person to test the elevator," Ellie protested.

"No, that wouldn't have been smart at all—but that doesn't make what happened okay. Engineering is supposed to *help* people, Ellie, and a good engineer should always put that first, even when she's very excited about a build. It's good that you thought to not use a person to test the elevator, but it would have been better if you'd taken your time, thought through the build, and tested it without someone else's things."

Ellie felt very small and very sad about this. She sniffed as her dad sat down on the barstool next to her, then clapped his hands on his knees. "So, what do you suppose we ought to do about this?"

Ellie chewed her lip. "Maybe . . . you could

help me build the elevator the *right* way?" she said. She hated just to give up on a project, after all, and her dad usually had good suggestions.

"That's a great idea," Ellie's dad said, and she brightened. "But what do you suppose we ought to do about your punishment?" he added, lifting an eyebrow.

"Right," Ellie said, sighing. She swung her legs back and forth hard on the barstool, thinking it over. Ellie's parents were big fans of her thinking up her own punishments—they said she had "such a good imagination, after all." Ellie had tried plenty of times before to suggest punishments like "only cinnamon buns to eat for a week!" or "real tracing paper to make blueprints!" but her parents never fell for it. Ellie told them it was because they lacked imagination.

"Maybe . . . I'm grounded?" Ellie suggested.

"That's not very interesting," Ellie's dad said, running his hand over his chin as if he had a beard (he didn't). "Hmm, what if–ah!" he said, putting a finger in the air. This is the same motion he made when he had a great engineering idea, but Ellie suspected that wasn't the case just now. "Ellie Bell, since your elevator project was very *not* helpful, for the next week your projects need to be *very* helpful."

Ellie's eyes widened. "That's it? I can do that!" she said.

"I know you can," Ellie's dad said. "And I know Mrs. Curran will *really* appreciate it."

Ellie stared. "Mrs. Curran?"

"You know–our neighbor at the end of the cul-de-sac," her dad said.

Ellie nodded. She knew who Mrs. Curran was but had never actually met her. She was a grandma-age lady who had a very proper garden out front. Grandma-age people were usually nice, Ellie knew, and they usually made cookies or lemonade and smelled like fabric softener. Helping out Mrs. Curran for a week sounded easy-peasy.

"She asked me to recommend someone to do a few small tasks around the house for her. I think you'll do a great job," Ellie's dad said, smiling some more. "You'll help out Mrs. Curran till Friday. And you won't eat pickles for the rest of the summer."

"No pickles is part of my punishment?" Ellie asked.

Her dad shook his head. "No—it's just that I don't think I can stand the smell of pickle juice ever again after today."

Chapter Three

The next morning, Ellie put on a tidy shirt, one with three buttons at the collar, and shoes with laces instead of flip-flops—grandma-age people always liked it when she wore tidy clothes. She brushed her hair straight (or tried to, anyway) and put it into a tight ponytail, then buckled on her tool belt. She'd spent all night thinking about things Mrs. Curran might need, like a lotion-bottle squeezer or a spinning tray that organized different sorts of cookies (she already had an idea for those things) or maybe something that automatically organized jewelry. Ellie didn't have enough jewelry to even have an idea for that one, but grandma-age ladies always did.

"Oh, you look very nice!" Kit said when Ellie met her at their fence. She'd told Kit about the punishment last night via walkie-talkie—they each had one in their bedroom. Kit was, of course, going to help Ellie at Mrs. Curran's—that's what best friends did. Kit had also dressed up in a very tidy outfit: she was wearing a pink fluffy skirt and shoes with little heels and giant heart-shaped rhinestones on the top.

"Thank you," Ellie said, and held out her notepad so Kit could see what she'd drawn that morning—ideas for the lotion squeezer and cookie organizer. Ellie always drew new

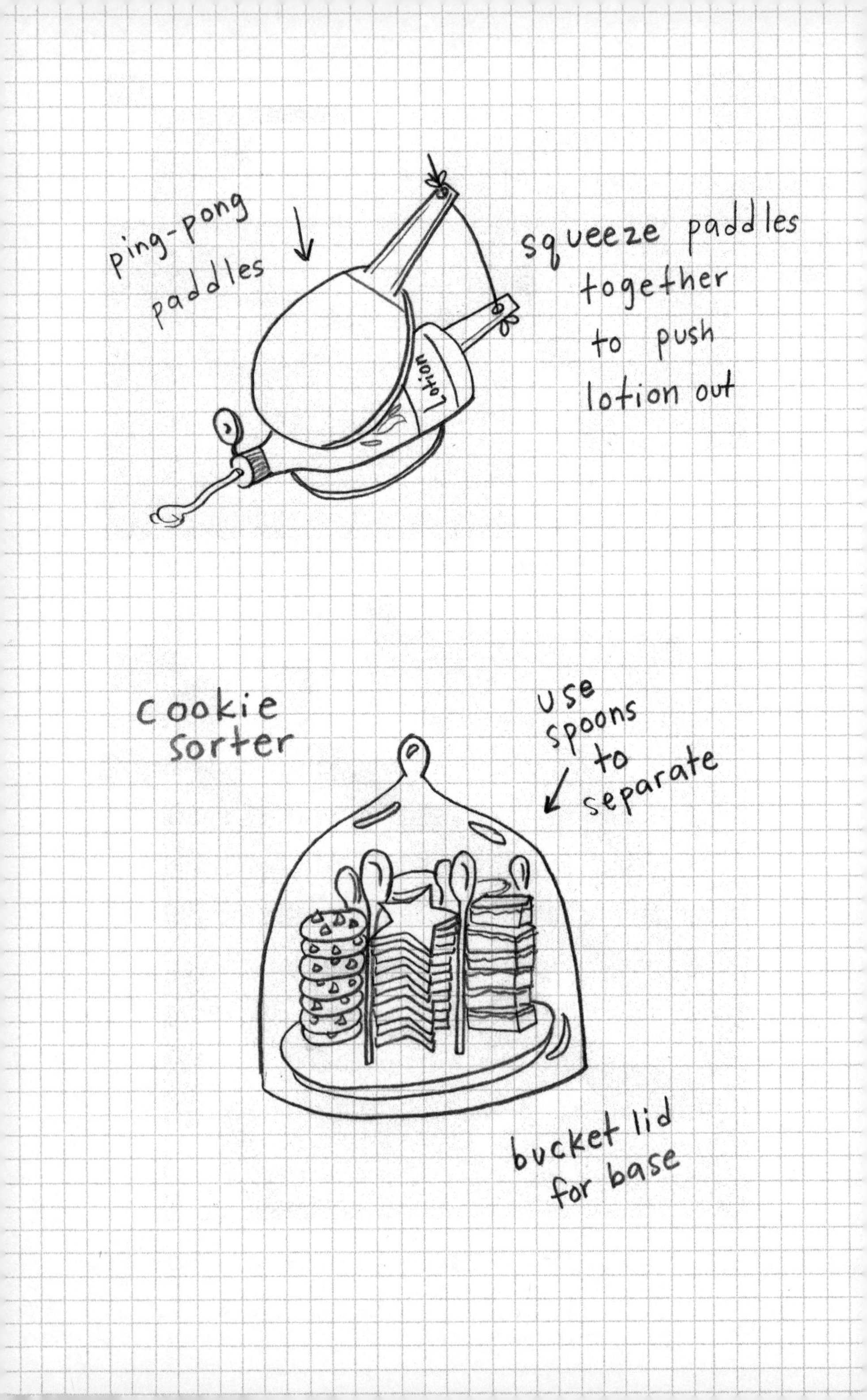
ping-pong paddles
squeeze paddles together to push lotion out
Lotion
cookie sorter
use spoons to separate
bucket lid for base

ideas in her notepad before she started building them so she could figure out all the tricky parts beforehand.

"These look great!" Kit said, her heels *click-clack*ing on the pavement as they walked toward the end of the cul-de-sac. "I bet Mrs. Curran will love them. I know my grandma would."

It was still early, and for a moment Ellie worried that Mrs. Curran wasn't even awake yet—her curtains were drawn tight and her garage was shut, and didn't people her age sleep late? The front yard wasn't a yard at all, but a garden with little stone paths through it and neat, orderly patches of flowers. There wasn't a single droopy or brown flower in the whole yard, as far as Ellie could tell. It looked like a picture, but probably not the kind of picture Ellie would want to hang in her room. Ellie was about to comment on this to Kit when the front door opened.

"Hello there, Ellie! Your father told me you'd be coming over to help me today," Mrs. Curran called across the garden to them, hands folded together at her waist, like she was welcoming them to a party.

"Hi, Mrs. Curran," Ellie and Kit said back at the exact same time. They looked at one another. Mrs. Curran was *not* what they expected. She was wearing high heels and makeup and even a little pearl bracelet and about a million rings on each finger. Her hair was long and straight and silvery-gray, and she was tall and lean like some of the flowers in the garden.

"Well, come along. Mind the flowers, please. Stay on those bricks," Mrs. Curran said, motioning to the path that cut through the garden and to her front porch. Ellie and Kit hopped along the bricks and to the front porch. This close, Ellie could tell that Mrs. Curran was wearing perfume—fancy spicy perfume, not baby powder the way other grandma-age people did.

"I'm so glad you've come to help out," Mrs. Curran said, then tilted her head to the side. "What sort of belt is that?" she asked, pointing to Ellie's tool belt.

Ellie looked at Kit. Kit raised an eyebrow (which was a skill she'd inherited, according to Toby, because not everyone can do that—like rolling your tongue). "It's my tool belt, Mrs. Curran," Ellie said carefully. Wasn't it obvious? It was a belt covered in tools, after all.

"A tool belt. Well. How nice," Mrs. Curran said in a way that told Ellie she didn't think it was nice, so much as weird. Except . . . why *wouldn't* Ellie need her tool belt, if she was here to help Mrs. Curran out? What was going on, exactly?

"Come on in—and please wipe your feet. Actually, perhaps you'd better take your shoes off entirely," Mrs. Curran said, glancing down at their feet. They obeyed, leaving their shoes on the front porch. They stepped through the door and into Mrs. Curran's house, and—

"Oh!" Kit said gleefully.

"Oh!" Ellie said only a little gleefully.

Mrs. Curran's house looked like a museum. A *doll* museum.

There were dolls on shelves, behind glass, sitting on fancy carved benches. The floor was covered in thick red rugs and the lights were all gold and flickery. The windows were covered in lacy curtains, which meant it was sort of dark, though ahead Ellie did see a patio door that led to a bright green back garden. There was a doll sitting on the bench out there.

"Look at the dolls!" Kit said, grasping Ellie's hand.

"I am!" Ellie answered. How could she *not* look at the dolls? They were everywhere!

"Yes, yes—*look* at the dolls. But please don't touch. They're very expensive," Mrs. Curran said sternly, shutting the door behind them.

"Why do you have so many?" Ellie asked.

"I paint them. That's my job—painting their faces and skin and hair. See? These are some I did," Mrs. Curran said, motioning to a case by the stairs. The dolls were on stands and had eyes that looked so real, they gave Ellie the heebie-jeebies. They were nothing at all like the dolls she had at home—those dolls could be tossed around or have their hair cut or accidentally get left at the theme park. These dolls definitely didn't visit theme parks.

"They're beautiful," Kit breathed.

"It's your *job*?" Ellie asked. It seemed like a strange job, and it was also a little weird to her that Mrs. Curran had a job at all. Her grandma didn't have a job, and neither did Kit's.

"It is," Mrs. Curran said warmly, and it was

clear she was very proud of her job. “Now, come with me.” Mrs. Curran swept around, walking in that quick way that adults walk when you’re meant to follow them. Ellie and Kit had to jog to keep up as they went down the hall. “Here’s what I thought you could help me with today–I need all of these envelopes stuffed. They’re bills for dolls I’ve painted,” she said when they reached the door to the kitchen.

It was one of those things where Ellie didn’t totally understand what Mrs. Curran was saying until she *saw* what Mrs. Curran was talking about. The kitchen table, which overlooked the backyard garden, was *covered* in paper and envelopes. You couldn’t even see the tabletop! They were all in neat stacks, but there were just *so many stacks.*

“Putting these in envelopes?” Ellie asked, surprised.

“Yes,” Mrs. Curran said politely. “Is that a problem?”

"It's just . . . um . . ." Ellie licked her lips and turned to Kit. Kit was better at talking to adults; Ellie gave her a *look*. Since they were best friends, when one gave the other a *look*, they could understand each other without talking out loud. Like when Kit gave Ellie a *look* that said "I need a snack *right now*," or Ellie gave Kit a *look* that said "stand back because this build might explode."

Kit nodded slowly at Ellie, then said to Mrs. Curran, "I think we were just expecting something a bit more . . . hands-on. Ellie is a great builder. She has plans for a cookie spinner, to organize the different types of cookies you make."

"Oh," Mrs. Curran said, chuckling a little. She put a ring-covered hand to her chest and smiled. "That's very sweet, but I don't make cookies. Though are you asking because you're hungry? I have some hummus in the fridge, if you'd like a snack."

She doesn't make cookies? Ellie thought, trying not to let the surprise show on her face. She had never met a grandma-age lady who didn't make cookies, and Ellie didn't even know what hummus was.

"We're not hungry, Mrs. Curran. But thank you," Kit answered for herself and Ellie.

"All right then—well, anyhow, I'll be in my studio working, should you need me. It's just up the steps, the first door you see."

And then, with another very nice but very lipstick-y smile, Mrs. Curran swept away, leaving Kit and Ellie with a pile—no, a *mountain*—of envelopes and absolutely nothing to engineer.

Chapter Four

Stuffing envelopes wasn't the *most* boring thing Ellie had ever done, but it was probably the second or third most boring. The first most boring was definitely the time Ellie's parents took her with them to the pottery store to buy planters and spent hours and hours and hours and hours looking at planters even though *they were just planters* so what was there even to look at for so long? Kit was better at being patient than Ellie was, and she calmly swung her legs back and forth under the chair while they worked. Ellie mostly squirmed.

"Look," Ellie whispered, jutting her chin toward the kitchen. "I could make a little wedge to stick under that door and keep it from being half-shut-half-open. That's helpful."

"But she asked us to stuff these envelopes," Kit said in a voice that sounded very grown-up.

"Ugggggh," Ellie said, and sank down in the chair. She put another boring invoice in another boring envelope, thinking about how much better it would be if she were in her workshop, thinking through what went so wrong with the elevator—she'd been working on a new design for it, but still hadn't worked it all out yet. Ellie grumbled, "I just thought we'd be building, that's all."

"I guess she just doesn't need help with building," Kit said, shrugging, then leaned back in her chair so she could see into Mrs. Curran's studio. "I wonder what she's painting. I wish she needed help with *that*."

"You'd be good at it," Ellie said, nodding.

"I didn't know there were real people who painted doll faces. I thought it was all machines," Kit admitted.

"Maybe I could make her a machine to—"

"Ellie," Kit said sternly.

"Uggggh," Ellie said again, and sank so far down that her eyes were even with the table.

"Everything all right in there?" Mrs. Curran called out. Ellie jolted back upright and stuffed envelopes faster than before.

"Yes, Mrs. Curran!" Ellie and Kit answered in unison.

It took almost two hours to put all the invoices into envelopes. The second the last paper was stuffed, Ellie leaped to her feet, called out "Thanks!" to Mrs. Curran, and sprinted for the front door. Kit hurried behind her, though she definitely took a little longer since she stopped to look at the dolls again on her way out.

"Free!" Ellie said, and cartwheeled on the sidewalk. Her hammer fell out of her tool belt, and she scrambled to get it.

"Oh, it wasn't so bad," Kit teased, though she was stretching her arms up to the sky—sitting for so long made them feel crunched up. "Wonder what she'll have us do tomorrow."

"Let's worry about that tomorrow," Ellie said with a sigh. "Come on, let's go find Toby."

Toby was in his front yard along with the other neighborhood boys—the McClellan twins and Dylan—playing some kind of game that looked like tag at first, but then looked like wrestling, and then looked like cowboy make-believe, and then looked like Dylan trying not to cry because he'd skinned his knee a little bit.

"It'll be fine. You just need to wash it off," Kit said matter-of-factly, as they all circled up around Dylan.

"It is fine! I don't care about it," Dylan said, but he was sniffling. Kit rolled her eyes at how hard Dylan was pretending it didn't hurt, then helped him up and led him into Toby's house.

"Tell my mom it wasn't my fault, Kit!" Toby yelled after them. Kit gave him a thumbs-up over her head. Toby turned to Ellie. "What happened after I left yesterday? Did your dad get the pickle jars cleaned up? Did the pickle juice kill the grass like I said it would?"

"I don't know about the grass. But my punishment is I have to help Mrs. Curran all week.

I thought that meant building things, but Kit and I just spent all morning stuffing envelopes," Ellie explained.

The McClellan twins and Toby all made the same "ew, gross" face.

"What did you guys do this morning?" Ellie asked. "Did I miss anything great?" A few weeks ago her parents had made her go shopping for new sandals, and she'd missed seeing a snake sleeping in a tree in Dylan's backyard. They'd tried to describe it to her (they said it was all lumped together like ice cream from a soft-serve machine) but it just wasn't the same, and then the snake was gone by the time she got home, and she'd lost one of the sandals at the pool anyway.

"We were waiting for you!" Toby said. "We were wondering if you know how to build a water park. Or at least a waterslide."

Ellie considered this. "Well, I don't really

know how to build anything that I haven't built before. You plan something and then you build it and then you know how after." This was something Toby still had trouble understanding—that Ellie could start building without knowing one-hundred-percent-for-sure how it would turn out. It seemed to impress him and also to make him sort of nervous.

"Do you think you know how to *plan* a waterslide? I had some ideas to start—here, come look," Toby said, waving for her and the McClellan twins to follow him.

They walked around to Toby's backyard, where there was a big blue camping tarp lying on the ground with a hose thrown over it. Everything was more than a little soggy, and it didn't look very water-slide-like.

"We put this down to slide on, and then put water on it, but we didn't slide very well," Toby said, frowning.

One of the McClellan twins cleared his throat and said, “We didn’t slide *at all*. That’s how I got this bruise. And that one. And that one.”

“We stopped when I got this one,” the other McClellan twin said, and pointed to a fat, purply bruise on his elbow.

Ellie cringed—it looked like it hurt. “Let me think,” she said, and walked in a big circle around the failed waterslide before pulling out her notepad. She drew a quick sketch of what she thought might work better.

She figured the best thing to do was to put the tarp up on the slide of Toby’s swing set. That way, they’d be sliding *down* for the first part, which would make them faster once they got to the flat part of the tarp. She also drew up a stand for the hose, so that it would spray water down the tarp the whole time.

“Ooo, that looks fun!” Kit said, reappearing

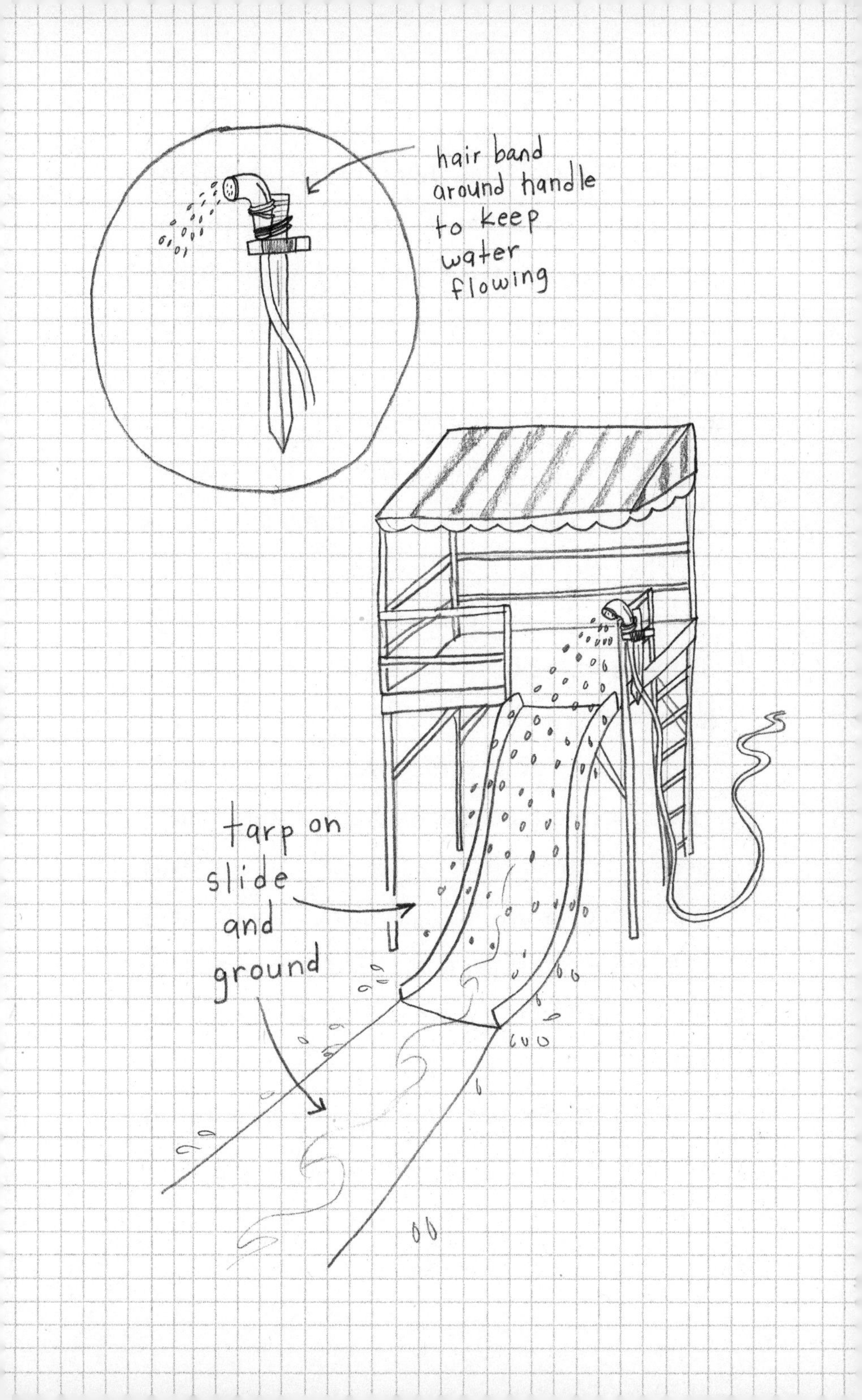
hair band
around handle
to keep
water
flowing
tarp on
slide
and
ground

behind Ellie. Dylan had seven robot Band-Aids on his knee. This was way more than he needed to cover the scrape, but he didn't look sniffly anymore, so Ellie figured they must be helping somehow.

"No waterslide robot?" one of the McClellan twins said when he spied over her shoulder, sounding more than a little disappointed.

"No, but this is still a machine, you know, just a really simple one," Ellie said helpfully, pointing to the slide. "Same as a ladder, or a ramp, or even stairs—they all connect something high to something low!"

"I *told* you a waterslide robot didn't make sense," Toby hissed at the McClellan (who looked like he still thought it was a good idea).

"Anyway," Ellie said. "How about you all get the tarp moved, while I work on the hose stand?"

"Got it!" Kit said cheerfully. Kit got everyone moving the tarp. Ellie, meanwhile, found a toy sword in Toby's garage, and stuck it in-between the wooden planks at the top of the swing set. She then balanced the hose on the handle part of the sword.

"But won't someone have to stand up here and squeeze the sprayer to make it work?" Dylan asked as the other boys and Kit stretched the tarp out nice and flat on the little hill.

"Nope! I thought of that," Ellie said, and took a hair tie out of her tool belt. Tool belts were for *all* kinds of tools, including hair ones. Plus it was really hard for Ellie to hammer things when her hair got in her face, which it almost always did even *with* a hair tie. She wrapped the hair tie around the sprayer so it held the trigger down, and water sprayed out the end in a big fan. It caught the light and made a little rainbow in the air.

"Is it ready?" Toby asked eagerly, rubbing his hands together.

"Almost–we need some soap," Ellie said.

"Soap? I think you only need soap with a real shower, not an outside shower," one of the McClellan twins said politely.

"It'll make it even slipperier, so we slide better," Ellie explained.

"Oh! It will lower the *friction*," Toby said, looking excited that he knew the word, even though Toby was the kind of person who always knew the word. "That's what it's called—friction. Friction makes it hard for things to slide."

He hurried inside and came back with a giant bottle of lemon-smelling soap—the kind for dishes. He squirted it all across the tarp; little bubbles fluffed into the air, and everything smelled lemony.

"*Now* it's ready," Ellie said, folding her arms. She couldn't wait to try it, but she was still a little slow to take off her tool belt. She didn't like taking off her tool belt—it was such an important part of her! It felt like taking off her legs or her elbows, but probably not exactly like that since it didn't hurt. It was just hard, is all. Ellie finally took the tool belt off, though, and laid it in a neat pile near Toby's deck.

"Come on, Kit—let's go together!" Ellie said. Kit nodded, and they climbed up to the top of the slide and then sat down one after another.

"Try not to go super fast. I don't want to end up in the mud at the end," Kit said so that just Ellie could hear. Kit was a very neat person, but sometimes she was shy about that.

"Okay—it's not mud, though, just grass. And we're sliding in soap and water, so it's basically exactly like the washing machine."

"I don't usually get *in* the laundry machine, though," Kit said, but she turned toward the waterslide anyhow. "Ready?"

"Go!" Ellie said, and she and Kit pushed off from the slide. They whizzed down the slide and shot out onto the tarp over the grass faster, faster, faster, until they slowed and rolled into a pile at the end of the ride.

The neighborhood boys whooped behind them; Ellie and Kit untangled their legs and high-fived.

"See? You *did* get to build something today after all!" Kit said, laughing, as they ran back to the top of the slide, ready for another turn.

They all ran back and forth and back and forth until everyone smelled like lemons and they'd all given up getting the little flecks of wet grass off their faces. It was pretty much perfect, in fact, until Toby's mom popped out of the garage door and saw what was going on. Toby was just about to launch himself down the waterslide when he saw her. He tried to stop but instead just tripped over his own feet and clunked down the slide instead of whooshing.

"Hey, Mom!" he called out, waving from the mud.

"Tobias Michaels! Did you ask permission to use that kitchen soap for a waterslide?" she called out. She didn't seem *mad*, but she definitely seemed *annoyed.*

Everyone looked at the ground except for Toby. Ellie hated it when her friends got in trouble in front of her, especially when she had something to do with it. She thought about what her dad said—that engineering was supposed to *help* people—and her stomach went squiggly.

"Oh. I forgot," Toby said, sounding nervous. "I'm sorry. I don't think we used much. And I read online that you can add water to a bottle of soap to make it last longer. It's a great budgeting tip!"

Toby's mom sighed, and when Ellie peeked her eyes up, she was relieved to see that

Ms. Michaels looked a teeny bit less annoyed. "Thank you for the tip, Toby, but that's not the point. We've talked about asking permission. Remember? I've told your brothers they can't use your things without asking anymore, Toby, and *they're* following the rules . . . How would you feel if they weren't?"

"Not very good," Toby said glumly.

"Well, you know the rule. Let's talk about a punishment after dinner," Ms. Michaels said, sighing.

"Ms. Michaels?" Ellie said, looking up. "I got in trouble earlier this week–"

"Yes, the pickles, I heard. Or I *smelled*, rather. Pickles do smell awfully strong in this heat."

"Yes, well, my punishment is helping Mrs. Curran all week. If that was Toby's punishment too, I bet we could be *really* helpful to her."

Ms. Michaels looked unconvinced, and so did Toby, actually—probably because they'd told him earlier about stuffing all those envelopes and how boring it was. But being punished together with your friends had to be better than being punished alone, right?

Finally, Ms. Michaels nodded. "All right, all right. Fine," she said, and walked down the driveway to get the mail. "And while you've got the hose running, water the begonias, please!"

"Happy to, Mom! Whatever I can do to help!" Toby said in a very too-chipper voice. He spun around to face the others, looking relieved. "Do any of you know which of these plants are begonias?"

Chapter Five

Ellie felt good about today. Maybe it was because she'd had so much fun on the water-slide the afternoon before, even though Toby had gotten in trouble. Or maybe it was because they'd had the not-shell-shaped boxed macaroni for dinner last night, which was Ellie's favorite. *Or* because last night while she was falling asleep she'd had some good ideas about her elevator design and had even thought to write them down before she conked out completely. It was probably all those things—*and* the fact that both Toby and Kit were going with her to Mrs. Curran's house today. More friends meant more fun, usually.

Besides, there were no more envelopes to stuff, so no matter what happened, today would be better than yesterday.

"Oh! You've brought another friend," Mrs. Curran said when she opened her door. She was sipping something hot out of a teeny cup and was wearing high heels again.

"Toby Michaels. A pleasure," Toby said, jutting his hand out in a very Toby way. Mrs. Curran looked charmed—people always looked charmed when Toby did this—and shook his hand politely.

"Is that a doll teacup? It's so tiny and cute!" Kit said, pointing to Mrs. Curran's cup.

"No, this is an espresso." Mrs. Curran chuckled. It must have been obvious they didn't understand, because she added, "It's a fancy coffee."

"Ohhhhh," the three of them said together, even though it still seemed pretty bizarre to Ellie that a grandma-age person drank a fancy coffee instead of tea.

"Well—how can we help you today, Mrs. Curran?" Ellie asked, then hurried on to say, "I brought my tool belt over again, so maybe if you need something—"

"I see that! I do have quite a big job for you this morning, so it's good you brought some friends," she said, turning and walking toward the kitchen. Ellie thought they were being led to the kitchen table again, and she could practically taste the envelope glue on her tongue at the memory of yesterday. Instead, Mrs. Curran opened a door to her garage. It was a very tidy garage, with all the lawn tools hung up on hooks and not a single dead bug in the corners. Up against the door were lots and lots of boxes addressed to Mrs. Curran.

"These are some of my painting supplies. It's tricky for me to get these upstairs, with my arthritis. They're just so heavy," Mrs. Curran said. "I hoped perhaps you could carry this pile to my studio for me?"

Ellie tried not to let her disappointment show that they *still* weren't building anything. Hey, it was better than stuffing envelopes, at least! "Of course we can, Mrs. Curran," she said.

"Excellent," Mrs. Curran said with a smile. "Now, can I offer anyone an espresso? Oh, hmm, probably shouldn't. Children don't drink espresso, do they?"

"Not regularly," Toby said.

"Perhaps some . . . some sparkling water, then? When you've finished?" Mrs. Curran suggested. Ellie had no idea what sparkling water was, but sparkly things were usually great, so she nodded and then they all got to work hefting boxes into their arms. They were the sort of boxes that were just heavy enough that you could carry only one at a time—and some were so heavy they took two people. Mrs. Curran was hard at work in her studio each time they walked upstairs, her paintbrush flashing over doll faces. She even painted little toenails and fingernails on the dolls! It was hard not to stop and watch, especially for Kit, who was very good at painting. When they had art class on Wednesdays at school, her pictures always got hung right at the front of the hallway.

"You have a very cool job, Mrs. Curran," Ellie said as she put down a box. Mrs. Curran was just finishing up a doll with light brown skin and a purple dress that looked like it would twirl really well. Ellie was a little jealous, since twirling dresses were the best sorts of dresses.

"Thank you, dear. I do love it so much–I get to play with dolls all day!" Mrs. Curran said, laughing a little at herself. "It's difficult to keep working, of course. With my studio being up here, I have a hard time getting things up and down the stairs."

"Dolls *do* seem to need an awful lot of things," Toby said as he rounded the corner with another box and set it down on top of all the others.

Mrs. Curran nodded. "Yes. Different paints, and wigs, and glues, and brushes, and pieces, and then of course I have to ship them back out, so there are boxes that must go back *downstairs* sometimes."

"What if you moved your studio to a room downstairs?" Kit asked–she'd arrived just behind Toby. "We could help you move it there!"

Mrs. Curran smiled at them. "That's very sweet, but the light is best up here. Light is very important when you're painting, and no light bulb is ever as good as the sunshine, if you ask me."

"They make special lights that are like the sun," Toby said, leaning on the doorframe. "People in Alaska use them because during the winter the days are only four hours long there. That's because of the tilt of the earth."

"Aren't you clever! Well, perhaps that works for Alaskans, but I think I'll just stick with my studio up here. When it gets too hard to get upstairs, I suppose that will mean it's just time to retire." Mrs. Curran said this with a smile, but it was crinkly and you could see through it to how she was actually very sad. Ellie wondered what it would be like if she couldn't engineer anymore—and it made her feel the same kind of miserable that Mrs. Curran looked.

"Well!" Mrs. Curran said, sniffing and sitting up. "That's not today, since I have you three to help me! How many more boxes are down there?"

"A bunch–let's go, guys!" Kit said in her most everyone-be-cheerful voice. They headed back downstairs, and Ellie knew without asking that Kit and Toby were feeling as badly for Mrs. Curran as she was.

"Maybe we could come over and carry boxes up for her every week?" Toby suggested.

"What about when we go back to school? Or if we get the flu at the same time? That happened to me and Kit in kindergarten," Ellie said, shaking her head.

Toby heaved another box into his arms and took a few steps, then put it back down. "Whoa. This one is extra heavy. What's in it?"

"Eyeballs," Ellie said, reading the label on

the side. "Well, *doll* eyeballs. I guess a *lot* of doll eyeballs?"

Toby looked a little queasy at the thought of a lot of eyeballs, even if they were just doll eyeballs in a box. "I guess two of us will have to carry this one."

Ellie suddenly had an idea. "Or . . . we could build something to take more boxes upstairs at once." Ellie looked from side to side, seeing what sort of stuff Mrs. Curran had stored in the garage. Building materials were everywhere, if you just knew how to look. She spotted two long shovels and some paint-mixing sticks, which, of course, were stacked neatly, like they were slices of bread. Then she whipped out her notepad and began to sketch as fast as she could.

Toby was peering over her shoulder. "Hey, I've seen those before! They used one to bring in our new refrigerator when the old one stopped working. We had to eat all the ice

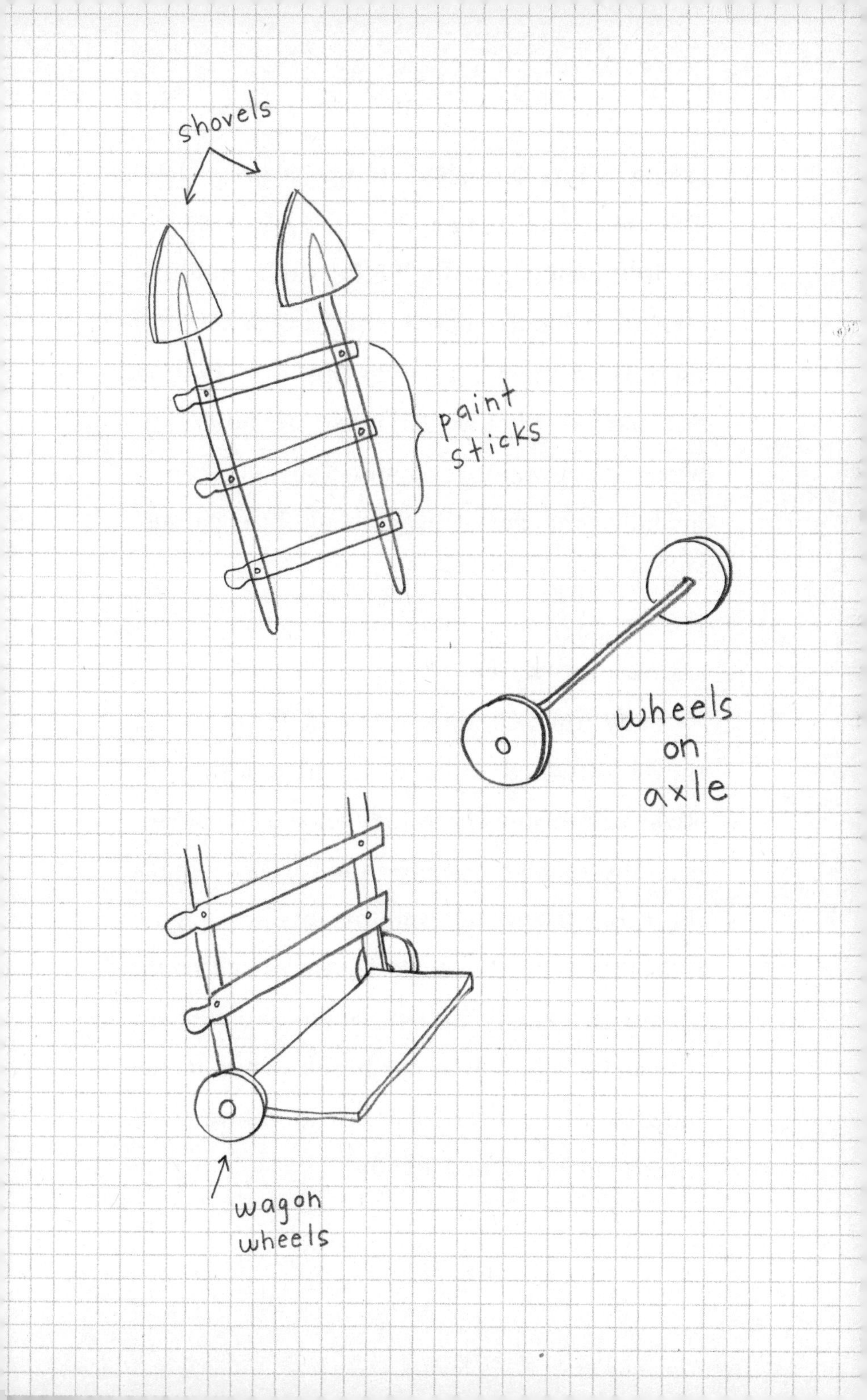
shovels
paint sticks
wheels on axle
wagon wheels

cream before it melted. It was a great day," Toby said, sighing happily at the memory.

"It's called a dolly," Ellie said, nodding. "We'll be able to stack the boxes up, then pull them from the garage right up to the bottom of the stairs. I bet we can make one quick, but we need a few more supplies. Toby, you run to my house and get the wagon out of the garage. Kit, go look in the workshop and find a nice flat piece of wood. Something about the size of a grown-up's shoebox."

Toby and Kit took off, and by the time they'd returned, Ellie had nailed the paint sticks to the shovels so they looked like a ladder. She took the wheels and an axle—that's the thing the wheels spin on—off her wagon. Ellie had done this so many times she could practically do it in her sleep—she needed wheels for a bunch of her builds. Then it was hardly a whole after-school cartoon's worth of time before they had a dolly!

"This looks almost exactly like the fridgey we used!" Toby said, grinning.

"The what?" Ellie asked.

"The fridgey. The one we used to get the new refrigerator in?"

"Oh!" Ellie said, eyes going wide. "They aren't named after the thing you're moving. It's called a dolly if it's moving dolls *or* refrigerators."

"I think 'fridgey' was a really fun word though," Kit said helpfully, so Toby wouldn't be too embarrassed at his mistake. He only turned a little bit red, so it must have halfway worked.

They stacked boxes on the dolly—it held seven—and then rolled it into the house. They still had to carry the boxes up the steps, but it was a lot faster than carrying boxes all the way from the garage.

"Why, what in the world? Is this what all that noise was about?" Mrs. Curran said, one hand fluttering over her chest in alarm—but the *good* kind of alarm. Ellie had gotten pretty good at telling the *good* kind of alarm from the *very bad* kind of alarm when grown-ups were concerned.

"We made a dolly to get boxes up here faster. I bet we only have one more trip now," Ellie said proudly as she helped Toby and Kit unload.

"How clever!" Mrs. Curran said. She looked at Toby. "Did you learn how to use tools from your father?"

Toby looked at Ellie, confused. She shrugged—she had no idea why Mrs. Curran was asking Toby that question, either. Toby finally said, "I guess. Mostly Ellie learned from *her* dad, though."

Mrs. Curran nodded. "That's very nice indeed. Well, thank you so much. I'm so glad you brought Toby over, Ellie! With his dolly you've made quick work of those boxes."

Ellie's mouth dropped open, but it was like someone had sucked all the words right out of her brain. *His* dolly? It was *their* dolly! They'd made it together—and Ellie had designed it! Why did Mrs. Curran think Toby had made it? She wanted to ask, but all the words seemed to have flip-flopped right out of her brain, like a fish on the ground. Ellie looked over at Kit and Toby—it looked like all their words were flopping fish, too.

"Thank you, children. I guess if you're done with the boxes now, you can go for today. I'll see you tomorrow morning." Mrs. Curran waved them toward the door. They stepped out into her perfect garden, and she closed the door behind them.

Well, it was more important that the dolly worked, and the boxes were moved upstairs, wasn't it? And besides, she still got to *build* the dolly, which was what she'd really wanted

Chapter Six

Ellie, Kit, and Toby arrived at Mrs. Curran's house bright and early the next day. Mrs. Curran was drinking an espresso and wearing high heels again. Ellie couldn't help but wonder if she ever *stopped* wearing high heels. She really was unlike any grandma-age person Ellie had ever met.

Today, Mrs. Curran wanted them to help

by dusting the downstairs. She gave them some dusting spray and cloths and a *lot* of advice on how not to break the fancy porcelain dolls (like don't touch them too hard or too much or at all if you can help it), and then she went upstairs to her studio. Ellie hadn't seen Mrs. Curran going up the stairs before and noticed now that it took her quite a long time to get up there. Her ankles wobbled in the high heels, and she had to hold tight to the railing.

"It would be easier for her to go upstairs, I bet, if she didn't wear high heels," Ellie said very quietly.

"High heels are very hard to wear," Kit said solemnly. "Remember that time I fell in the Miss Peachy Keen Pageant? It was because my high heels were so high."

"Why do they make shoes that are so dangerous?" Toby asked, shaking his head. "Hey,

Ellie—maybe you could engineer her some better shoes!"

"I think she *likes* her high heels," Kit said, sounding a bit defensive. Ellie knew why—Kit really liked high heels, too, even though she'd fallen that one time. She just walked super carefully in them at pageants now.

"But even if you like them, why wear them all the time if it makes walking so much harder?" Ellie asked.

"You wear your tool belt almost all the time, even though it makes jumping on the trampoline so much harder," Toby pointed out thoughtfully.

Ellie frowned. That was true. Her tool belt was a part of her. Maybe high heels were a part of Mrs. Curran.

"Anyway," Ellie said, and pulled out her notebook. "I was thinking—Mrs. Curran really liked that we made that dolly yesterday, even though she didn't exactly ask us to make it. Maybe today we can do some other helpful things she didn't ask us for. After we finish dusting, I mean."

"Are you sure you don't just want to build something?" Kit asked, but she was just teasing. Though she was probably right. (Okay, she was definitely right.)

Ellie had a list of things she'd noticed around Mrs. Curran's house that needed fixing. None of them were builds, exactly–just repairs. Some crooked cabinet doors and some wobbly tables and some doors that didn't quite shut smoothly. Ellie didn't say it out loud, but she also reasoned that maybe Mrs. Curran would have an easier time believing Ellie was an engineer if they did *lots* of stuff around the house, instead of just one big thing like the dolly.

They dusted as fast as they could, which was

actually not very fast because Mrs. Curran had lots of fancy little objects on shelves that you had to be really careful around. And, of course, there were lots of dolls. Most of them were in cases, so they didn't need to be dusted, but some were out in the open and Kit, Ellie, and Toby were extra careful as they blew dust off their little doll heads. It was hard for Ellie not to play with them, and it *seemed* hard for Toby not to play with them, but it was clearly very, very, very, *very* hard for Kit not to play with them.

"This one is my favorite," Kit would say, but then a few minutes later, she'd say, "Wait, no, this one! Look at her pants! I think she's an explorer. Those look like explorer pants, I think. Oh, but look at that one over there!"

A little while later they were finally finished, so Ellie waved the list in the air eagerly. Together, they unscrewed the hinges on

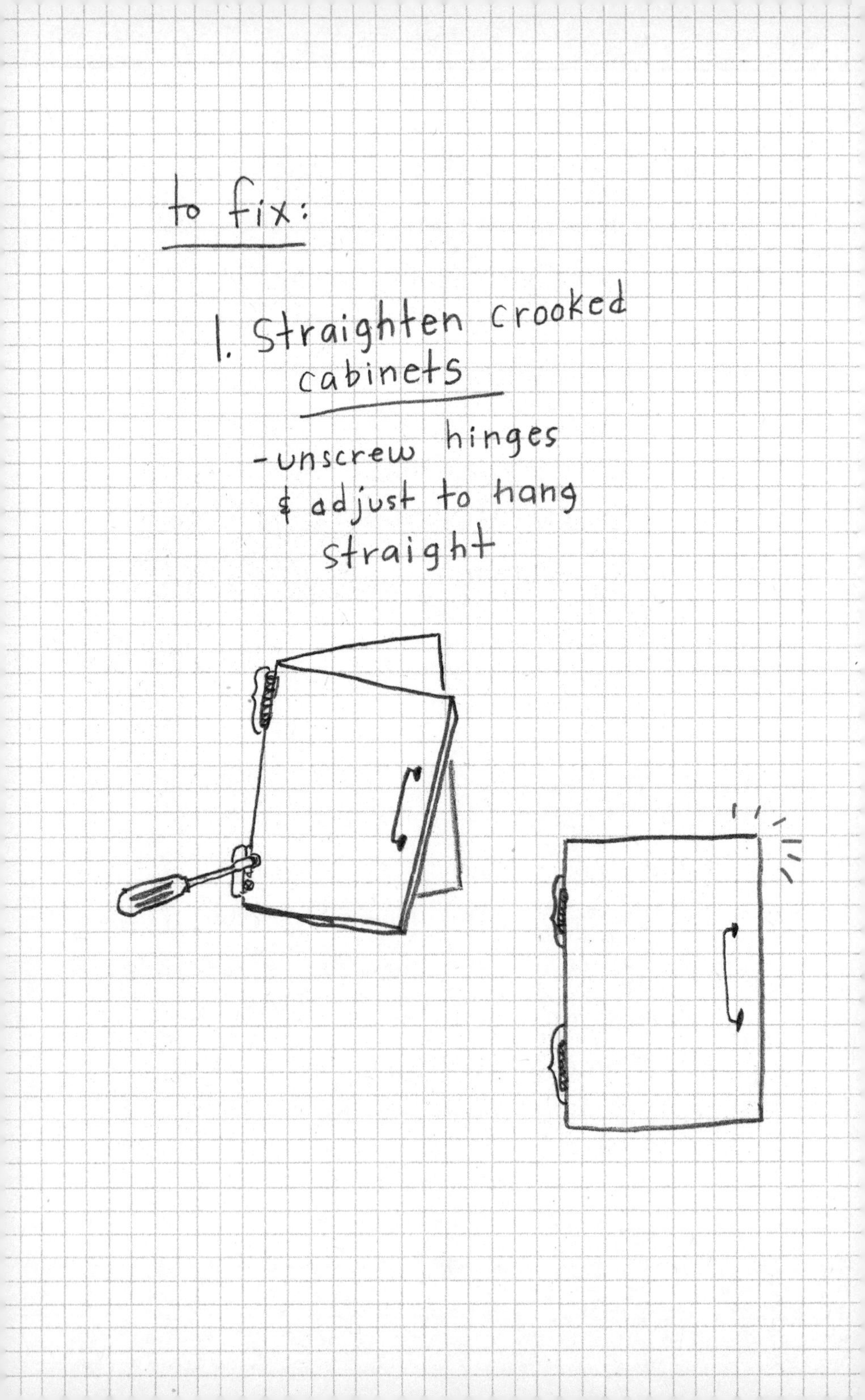
to fix:
1. Straighten crooked cabinets
-unscrew hinges
& adjust to hang straight

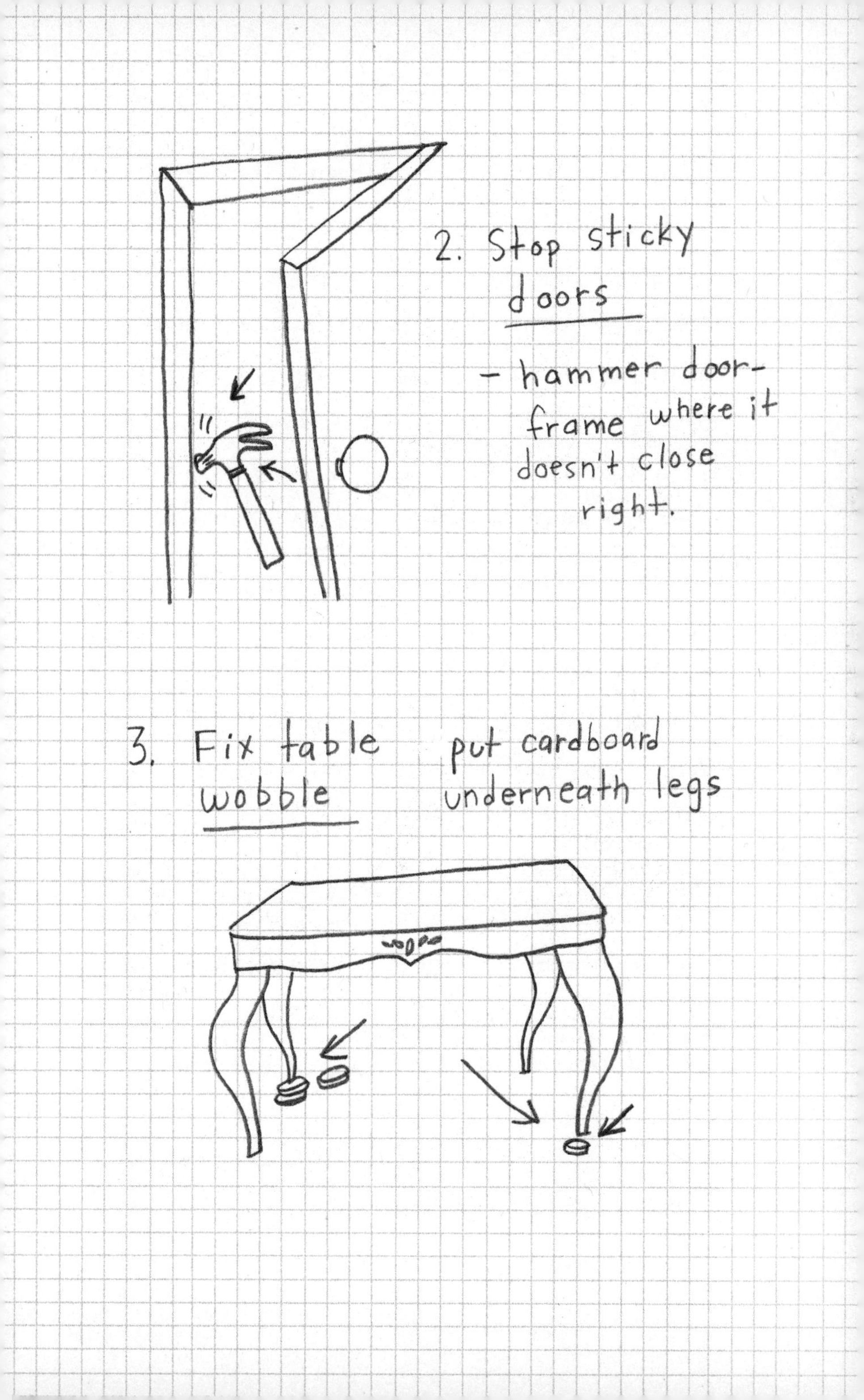
2. Stop sticky doors
- hammer door-frame where it doesn't close right.
3. Fix table wobble
put cardboard underneath legs

cabinet doors and adjusted them so they didn't hang crookedly. They hammered a bit on the frames of the doors that didn't close neatly to smash in the wood a little so there was more space for the door to swing. For the tables, Ellie asked Toby to cut some tiny circles out of a cardboard box. They pancaked them together, then stuck them under the table legs so everything was level.

"Let's go tell Mrs. Curran!" Ellie said proudly when they'd finished. Even though big builds were a lot of fun, sometimes it felt really good to finish lots and lots of little things like this.

"Tell me what?" Mrs. Curran asked from the bottom of the stairs. The three of them jumped in surprise, but then Ellie grinned.

"That we finished dusting! But we also did lots of other stuff to help you. See? Come look," she said, and waved Mrs. Curran over to one of the doll cabinets. "Remember how this door was crooked? We straightened it out!"

"So you did," Mrs. Curran said, looking impressed. "My goodness. I've never so much as held a hammer, and look at what you lot have managed!"

"Yes! *And* we also made the table in the kitchen not wobble," Ellie went on. "And the door that goes to the little bathroom shuts better now."

"You really did all that?" Mrs. Curran asked.

"Yes. I'm an engineer," Ellie said firmly. She felt a little bad, though, because it wasn't like Kit and Toby hadn't done all the work, too. She fixed it by saying, "I'm an engineer, but we all did the work."

Mrs. Curran was still marveling at how straight the doll cabinet door was, opening and shutting it several times. Finally, she looked up. “This is just wonderful. You know, I think—yes. Let’s see . . .” She slowly stooped down and opened one of the lower doll-cabinet doors, then reached inside. She rummaged around for a moment, then withdrew two dolls with braided black hair and bright eyes. She handed one doll to Kit, then the other to Ellie. Kit looked like she very truly might faint right then and there.

“For keeps?” Kit asked, eyes wide.

“Yes, yes. They’re plastic, not porcelain, so they aren’t quite as fragile as the ones I paint these days—but I think they’re lovely all the same,” Mrs. Curran said, smiling at them. She turned to Toby. “I’m afraid I don’t have any toys you would be interested in, Toby! It’s a pity that boys don’t play with dolls.”

Toby frowned—in fact, all three of them

frowned. Toby played with dolls plenty—in fact, he really liked it when they played tea party with Ellie or Kit's dolls. He knew all the rules about throwing fancy tea parties and which forks to use and never minded when the tea-party dolls suddenly became undercover spies who were only pretending to be at a normal tea party.

Toby looked at the ground, then over at Ellie's new doll a little sadly. Mrs. Curran must not have noticed, though, because she stood up and shut the cabinet doors. "I think it's very gentlemanly of you, Toby, to invite girls to help you build things. Plenty of boys wouldn't do that, you know, much less let a girl wear his tool belt."

Ellie's jaw dropped so far that she felt like one of those cartoon characters whose jaw literally hits the ground. Mrs. Curran thought her tool belt was *Toby's*? What?

"Oh, that's not mine," Toby said quickly. "That's Ellie's tool belt. Those are her tools."

"You have your own! How nice. Well, I need to get back to work, you three. Thank you so much for all your hard work today. I won't need you tomorrow, since I have a hair appointment, but I'll see you the day after. Toby, dear, I'll think of something for you—you deserve the biggest gift of all, what with all the repairs you did to my house!"

"But Mrs. Curran!" Ellie said loudly, shaking her head. What was going on? Mrs. Curran was so mixed up, but she didn't seem to realize it one bit—she was just smiling at them nicely, blinking, waiting for Ellie to keep speaking. But the words had all fallen from Ellie's brain, and she had no idea what to say, much less how to say it. She looked down at the doll in her hands and her eyebrows wrinkled together.

"Let's go, Ellie. We'll see you day-after-tomorrow, Mrs. Curran!" Kit said in a very calm, very Kit voice. She linked her arm with Ellie's and led her out of the house, with Toby following behind.

Chapter Seven

"It was *bonkers*!" Ellie said, and smashed her pillow against her head. She was still wearing her tool belt. She was supposed to take it off for bed, but her dad, who was sitting on the side of her mattress, hadn't said anything about it (yet). But after hearing what had happened with Mrs. Curran, her dad definitely understood why she didn't want to take it off, though, and why she was smashing her head with a pillow.

"It *was* bonkers," Ellie's dad answered, nodding. "That must have been very frustrating. It does sound like you were very helpful, though. That was nice of you to fix so many things in Mrs. Curran's house, when you could have just left after dusting."

"Yeah," Ellie said, removing her head from the pillow. Her hair was crazy and staticky on top of her head, like a baby bird's feathers. She sighed and turned over. "But it isn't fair."

"No, it isn't very fair," he said. "It's never fair when people make assumptions—like that you aren't an engineer, or that Toby wouldn't want a doll, or that I'm bad at basketball just because I'm short—"

"What?"

"Never mind that last one. It's never right to make assumptions about somebody," he said firmly. "Everyone is who they are, and who they are is perfect."

Ellie nodded. It was very nice to hear her dad say this, of course, because he was really smart, so Ellie knew it was true. Still, though, Mrs. Curran's thinking that Toby was the engineer was biting at her ankles. It wasn't exactly the first time someone had been surprised about Ellie's being an engineer—lots of times, grown-ups thought the tool belt was just for show or that she was only playing with her dad's tools. Ellie had always been able to prove them wrong, though, in the end.

"But why wouldn't Mrs. Curran believe me when I proved her wrong?" Ellie asked out loud. She hadn't said any of her other thoughts out loud, but her dad knew what she meant. She and her dad were sort of mind readers like that.

"Well, first of all, it is wrong of her to need

proof that you're an engineer." He took a big breath, then went on, "But sometimes people are like that. I think Mrs. Curran has just never met a girl who is an engineer—and a *good* engineer, who makes all kinds of useful things . . . with the exception of that pickle elevator."

"It wasn't a pickle elevator—the pickles were just *on* the elevator when it—" Ellie stopped short when it looked like her dad might be remembering that day a little too clearly. He cringed, and it looked like he was imagining the smell of all that pickle juice again. "Sorry," she said in a low voice. "Go on."

"Right—anyhow, maybe the problem is that Mrs. Curran thinks engineering is for other people."

"What do you mean?" Ellie asked, turning over. She'd been tossing and turning, and now her skirt *and* tool belt *and* body were all tangled up in her unicorn bedsheets. As her dad answered, he tried to help her get untangled.

"I mean that Mrs. Curran was a little girl once, too—she was your exact age, a long time ago. Maybe she never even *dreamed* of being an engineer. Maybe she doesn't really know what it is to be an engineer. Maybe even the idea of using a hammer is crazy—and that's just one teeny part of engineering! Maybe—Ellie, *how have you tied the quilt in a knot?*" he said, shaking his head at the cocoon of blankets Ellie had wrapped around herself.

Ellie scooched up in the bed and kicked her legs free from the blankets. Her dad was staring at the knot in the quilt in disbelief. He reached for one of the screwdrivers on Ellie's tool belt and jammed it into the knot to untie it. "Anyhow," he said. "Maybe Mrs. Curran never believed *she* could be an engineer, so she doesn't believe *you* could be an engineer."

Ellie considered this. "But no one is automatically an engineer. Everyone has to learn."

Her dad lifted his eyebrows at her, which meant he was waiting for her to realize something.

Ellie mashed her lips together. "So . . . you think that we need to teach Mrs. Curran to be an engineer?"

"Maybe," Ellie's dad said, nodding. "Maybe that's the best way to show her engineering is for everyone, and not just boys."

"That might be hard," Ellie said, imagining Mrs. Curran holding a hammer. It looked about as out of place as Kit holding a squid. Ellie knew Kit had never seen a squid outside of pictures, but they looked slimy, gooey, and sticky enough that she refused to go into the ocean over her head. Ellie had suggested an antisquid suit of armor but hadn't figured out how to build one that Kit could swim in (yet).

"It's always hard to change someone who has made an assumption," Ellie's dad said. "But the best way to change a person's mind is to teach them."

"Or maybe *you* could just tell her I'm an engineer?" Ellie suggested. "I bet she'll believe you. Grown-ups usually believe other grown-ups."

"Good night, Ellie," her father said, and kissed her forehead.

"But Dad—"

"*Butts* are for sitting on," her dad answered. "Don't sleep with the tool belt on. You'll get screwdriver-shaped bruises."

"Okay," Ellie grumbled as her dad clicked off her lamp.

She slept with her tool belt on anyway (mostly by accident), and even though she got screwdriver-shaped bruises, they were totally worth it.

Chapter Eight

"I don't know," Kit said thoughtfully, twirling her hair around her fingers.

"You didn't know a thing about engineering when we met," Ellie pointed out.

Kit frowned. "That's true. And neither did Toby. But Toby and I *wanted* to learn about engineering. I don't know that Mrs. Curran does. Oh—wait, let me grab her foot."

The foot in question belonged to Miss Penelope, Kit's pet sheep. Kit's dad and sister were allergic to dogs, so they'd gotten her a sheep for her last birthday. Sheep, as it turned out, made pretty good pets. Even if they couldn't be potty-trained, they *could* be trained to spin in circles, jump over broomsticks, and not steal carrot sticks right out of your hand. Miss Penelope was trying very hard to eat a patch of dandelions in Kit's yard, but Ellie and Kit were trying equally as hard to get a dog harness through her legs. Kit caught the sheep's foot and tucked it through the harness, then clipped the harness shut.

They were in the process of building a saddle for Miss Penelope's back—one that the dolls Ellie and Kit had gotten from Mrs. Curran could ride in together. The project was trickier than it sounded, since Miss Penelope (and, Ellie supposed, *all* sheep) sort of pranced when she walked. The prancing had made the saddle sway back and forth on Miss Penelope's back until the dolls jostled right out of their first few saddle attempts. Ellie had decided some research was in order–research was very, very useful for engineers, and so when the first few saddles hadn't worked, she'd looked up other sorts of saddles on Kit's mom's phone. Research was also sometimes very, very surprising, because the saddle that Ellie thought would work best for Miss Penelope was the type people used on elephants.

"All right, how do we build this elephant saddle?" Kit asked, plopping down on the ground as Ellie opened up her notebook.

"I was thinking something like this," Ellie said, and drew as fast as she could.

"See this piece here?" Ellie asked, pointing to the X-shaped bit at the bottom of the saddle. "I'm not sure what to build it out of, but I think that's the thing that keeps the

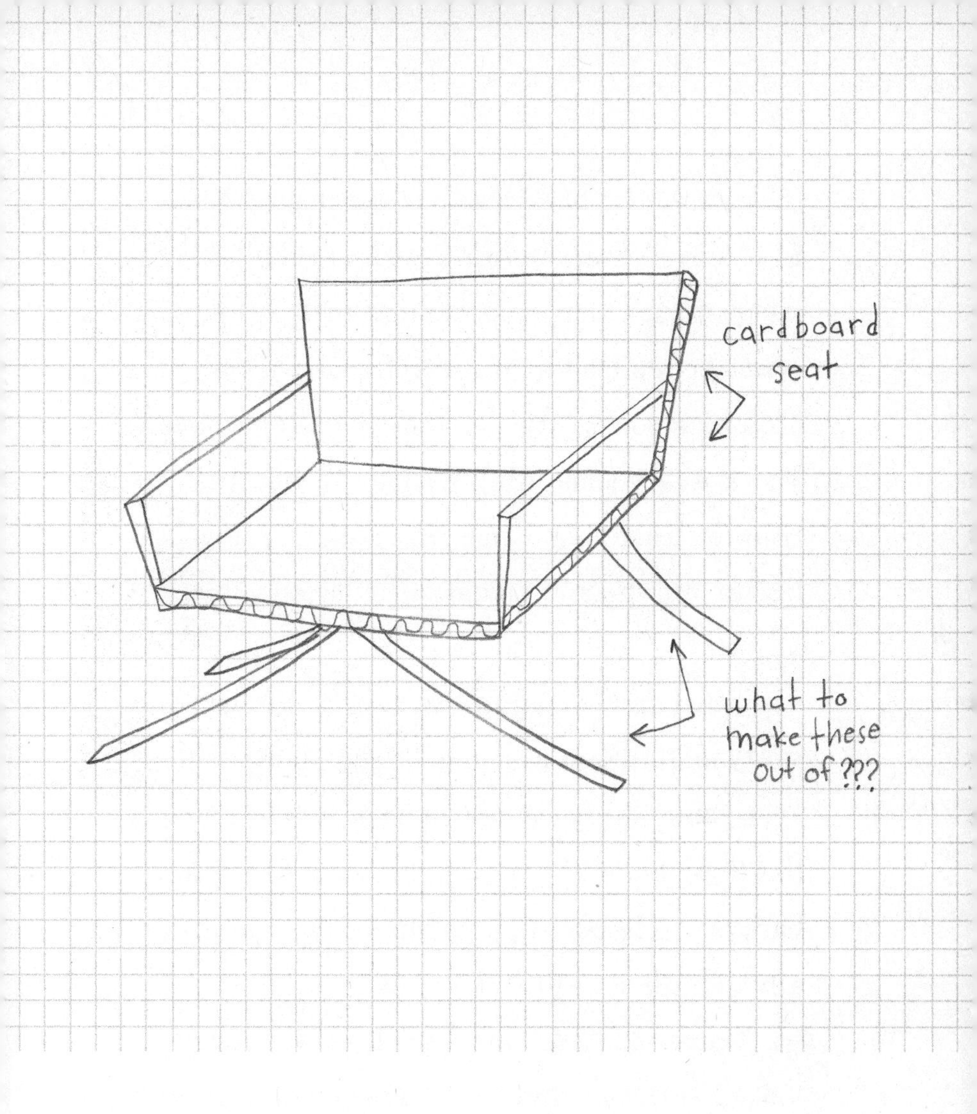

saddle steady when an elephant or a Miss Penelope is moving or prancing or jumping."

"Real elephants can't jump, though," a voice said—Toby's voice. He was standing at the gate to Kit's backyard, peering inside. When Ellie looked over, he slunk back, like he hadn't meant to say that loud enough to be spotted. When he realized they'd seen him, he added, in a quieter voice, "It's not that they don't have knees—that's something people say, but it isn't true. It's that they can't get enough spring to lift up into the air. And also they weigh, like, a *lot* a lot."

"What are you doing out there?" Ellie asked.

"You didn't invite me in," Toby pointed out, even though this was strange because it wasn't like Toby *had* to knock and be invited into the backyard. He could just come on in, and usually did, same as Ellie.

"Come in," Ellie said, and Toby did, but he looked at the ground a lot. "Are you all right?" Ellie asked.

"Yes."

"Are you sure? You don't look all right," Kit

said, hauling Miss Penelope back to where they were standing. (Miss Penelope could be a very stubborn sheep, so sometimes you really had to pull her along.)

Toby scratched Miss Penelope's head with his fingertips, then toed at the dirt when he answered. "Are you guys mad at me for yesterday? For what happened with Mrs. Curran thinking I did all the building? I thought you might be especially, Ellie."

Now it was Ellie's turn to toe at the dirt. She wasn't mad *at* Toby–it wasn't his fault, after all, and he'd tried to tell Mrs. Curran the truth. But she *was* still pretty mad about the situation.

"It wasn't your fault," Ellie finally said. "I'm not mad at you."

"Okay," Toby said, looking relieved. "I tried to tell her! And she didn't believe me, and then she didn't give me a doll." He looked especially sad at that last part, and Ellie could tell Toby was sadder than she's realized about not getting a doll.

"You can play with our dolls," Kit said helpfully. "We were just making them a saddle so they can ride on Miss Penelope like she's an elephant-sheep. A sheepephant?"

"An elepheep" Ellie suggested.

"A shelephant?" Toby said, and they all nodded, since that was clearly the best one.

Ellie showed Toby the sketch of the shelephant saddle and explained how they were having to think about what to use for the part at the bottom.

"I think on real elephant saddles, those bits are carved out of wood," Toby said, tilting his head to the side as he studied the drawing. "Can you carve wood?"

"I'm not allowed to use the good knives anymore," Ellie said, shaking her head. "Any other ideas?"

They tried quite a few things they could find at Kit's house—drinking straws (too flimsy), Popsicle sticks (not long enough), wire coat hangers (too pokey), and bananas (the right shape, but Miss Penelope ate them—peels and all—when no one was looking). They were all watching Miss Penelope nose at the last pieces of banana peel, when Ellie suddenly thought of what they could use. She jumped to her feet and dashed back to her house without saying anything, then returned a few moments later with . . .

"More dolls?" Kit asked, confused. Ellie had two of her old dolls in her arms. They weren't looking so great—Ellie and Kit had cut off their hair a little unevenly while playing salon, and one's face had gotten a *teeny* bit melted when Ellie got her too close to a hot glue gun.

"Are those for me? Because . . . um . . ." Toby asked hesitantly, looking between the not-so-great-looking dolls and the new dolls from Mrs. Curran.

"Look!" Ellie said, and held up one of the dolls. They were the sort of dolls with real joints—Ellie bent the doll's leg just a little bit at the knee.

"Oh!" Kit and Toby said in perfect unison.

They popped the legs off the dolls—Toby was pretty grossed out by this, but doll legs and heads came off so often that Ellie and Kit weren't fazed—and bent them just a teeny bit. They were *perfect* for the bottom piece of the saddle. They attached them to the cardboard piece, then attached that to Miss Penelope's harness.

"I don't know. It looks kinda creepy," Toby said.

"*Good* creepy," Kit said, giggling.

They placed their new dolls in the saddle and buckled them in with Kit's hair ribbon.

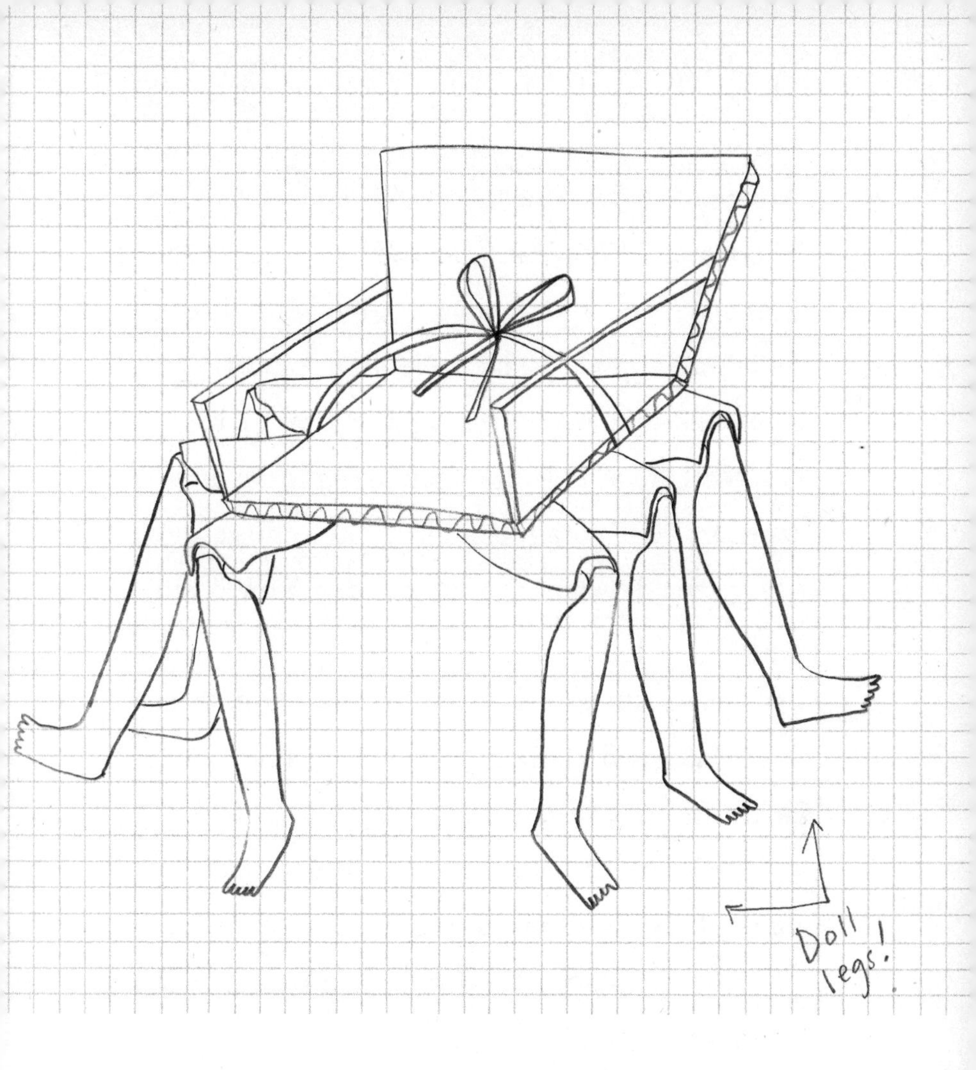

Then, Ellie led Miss Penelope very slowly forward to see if the saddle slipped at all . . .

"It works!" Toby shouted, pumping his fist in the air. This startled Miss Penelope, who bounced away, but the dolls stayed put in their seats! Ellie, Kit, and Toby clapped as she jumped over the fence around Kit's mom's blueberry bushes. The shelephant saddle kept the dolls safe, even through the jump.

"Kit! What is your sheep doing in my blueberries?" Kit's mom called through the screen door. "And—*what is that on her back*?" she shrieked.

"It's a shelephant saddle!" Kit said. Kit's mom stepped through the screen door, eyes wide and mouth parted in horror.

"Are your dolls riding on the *body parts of other dolls*?" Kit's mom asked.

"Just the legs," Ellie said. "And they were old dolls."

Kit's mom swallowed very hard, then shook her head. "I'm going to guess you made that, Ellie Bell?"

"We all made it," Ellie said.

"But it was Ellie's idea," Toby said proudly, knocking Ellie with his elbow.

"I guessed as much," Kit's mom said thickly. "Have you ever considered engineering *nice* things, Ellie? Like maybe . . . maybe a pretty doll bed? Or a chair to sit very still in?"

"Mom!" Kit said. "That's very rude! The shelephant saddle is very nice!"

"Apologies, apologies," Kit's mom said with a sigh, then turned to go back inside, grumbling under her breath. Kit was clearly embarrassed about what her mom had said, but Ellie was beaming. It felt so good that at least one grown-up knew she was an engineer.

Chapter Nine

"We can do this," Ellie said, nodding tightly as they stood at Mrs. Curran's door the next morning.

"Of course we can," Kit said, nudging her.

"I don't know," Toby said, shaking his head.

"Toby!" Kit and Ellie said at once, and glowered at him.

Toby grumbled. "Okay, okay. We can do it! I think. We might be able to do it."

"You're not being very supportive," Ellie said, folding her arms.

Toby sighed and gave a not-very-convincing thumbs-up.

Today was the day they were going to try to teach Mrs. Curran some engineering, and the truth was, Toby was saying exactly what Ellie was feeling—lots and lots of doubt that this was going to work. They'd come up with a plan yesterday afternoon, after playing with Miss Penelope for a few hours, but making a plan in Kit's backyard and going through with that plan at Mrs. Curran's house suddenly seemed like very, very different things.

"Stop it! You can't get on the pageant stage expecting to lose!" Kit said. She could see the worry on Ellie's face. She grabbed Ellie's shoulders and looked her dead in the eye, then said, "Chin up! Eyes and teeth! Smile big!"

This wasn't a pageant, and Ellie wasn't so sure that pageant tips were going to work, but she forced a smile all the same. Kit reached forward and rang Mrs. Curran's doorbell.

"There you are!" Mrs. Curran said when she answered. Today she was wearing a long skirt with feathery bits that fell down to her high heels, and a silky blouse. She sipped on her tiny espresso cup as she stepped aside to let them in. "You're a bit later than usual, and I had begun to think perhaps you weren't coming today. I'm so glad you have, though, because I picked up something for you, Toby!"

"Oh!" Toby said. It was obvious that Toby was mixed up—it was nice to hear she had a gift for him, but also it felt wrong to take one since Mrs. Curran was giving it thinking Toby had fixed up her house himself. Mrs. Curran clicked away in her heels to the dining room table, then turned around to hand him a bag from the store up the street. Toby reached into the bag and pulled out the present.

"Thank you so much, Mrs. Curran. This is great," Toby said, turning the gift over and over. It was a . . . box of sand? Toby looked at Ellie for an explanation, but she was just as confused as he was.

"It's an ant farm! I know little boys like bugs," Mrs. Curran said with a chuckle. "Now, you have to send off for the ants, but there's a little paper in there that shows you how to do it."

Kit, who was not really interested in bugs, looked like she might be sick over the idea of ants in the mail. Ellie wondered why anyone would *need* to send ants through the mail, when they were all over the yard anyway. Toby, however, looked a little more interested in the present now.

"Cool!" he said. "Does it come with instructions on how to teach the ants to farm? What do they farm?"

Mrs. Curran chuckled. "I think just dirt, dear. They make tunnels. Anyhow, today if you don't mind, I thought you might help—"

"Oh, wait!" Ellie jumped in. She'd almost zoned out, wondering about ants in the mail. She looked up at Mrs. Curran and thought about what Kit said—*Chin up! Eyes and teeth! Big smile!*

"We thought that today, Mrs. Curran, you might like to hold a hammer." Ellie said this as dramatically as possible, like she was saying, "You might like to have a billion dollars!" or "You might like to have this boat full of puppies!"

"I'm sorry?" Mrs. Curran asked, scrunching her brows.

"When we were here last time, you said you'd never held a hammer, and I think that's a real shame—hammering is easy! And fun! So I thought maybe you'd like it if we taught you how to hammer. Or maybe use a screwdriver? That way you don't have to wait around for someone to come fix things in your house, unless you just *want* to wait . . ." Ellie drifted off and went back to smiling so hard her cheeks hurt.

"Too much *teeth*," Kit muttered, and Ellie toned her smile down a notch.

Mrs. Curran tilted her head at Ellie. "Er—I don't think so, sweetheart. It's very nice that Toby has taught you and Kit to use a hammer, but I'm afraid I'd just wallop my fingers with it!"

Toby cleared his throat. "Actually, Mrs. Curran, Ellie taught *me* to use a hammer. She's an engineer. Kit and I just help out a lot."

Mrs. Curran's head tilted even *more* at that, like Toby was speaking a language she didn't understand. "Goodness, isn't that just . . . a girl engineer! Curious."

"Anyone can be an engineer, Mrs. Curran. Boys and girls and everyone in between!" Ellie said.

Mrs. Curran smiled and righted her head. It didn't look like she believed Ellie—it looked like she was doing that thing grown-ups do where they agree but secretly think you're being silly. She said, "Of course, of course. Well, thank you, but I don't think I need to learn to use a hammer. Whatever would I do with it?"

"All sorts of things!" Ellie said.

"Pull out nails," Toby said.

"Break the window into a billion pieces if you lock your keys in the car," Kit said.

"I think I would rather just call a locksmith, in that case," Mrs. Curran said delicately. "Anyhow, today I would love for the three of you to help me by scrubbing the patio stones. They're terribly mossy, and I worry I'll slip and fall on them when I go out to pick mint from my garden."

Ellie bit her lip. This wasn't going very well. They'd planned to teach Mrs. Curran to hold a hammer, then teach her how to use it to tap-tap-tap paint cans closed or put nails in the wall to hang pictures. A hammer was a pretty easy tool to use, and one of the handiest ones Ellie owned. Using one was only a tiny part of engineering, but it was a start!

"Are you sure you don't want to try to use the hammer, Mrs. Curran?" Ellie asked.

Mrs. Curran smiled nicely. "I just don't think that's very useful for me, dear. Besides, I don't know a thing about tools or engineering!"

Ellie wanted to point out that if she learned to use a hammer, then she *would* know a thing about tools and engineering, but it was clear they weren't getting anywhere. The three of them went outside and began to scrub at the patio with thick scrub brushes and hot water; Mrs. Curran started her slow climb up the steps to her studio.

"I knew we couldn't do it," Toby said grumpily once Mrs. Curran was out of earshot.

"Me too," Ellie said sadly.

"Me three," Kit added. Ellie and Toby looked over at her, and she shrugged. "Mom says that at pageants you have to *fake it till you make it*. That's what I was doing—just pretending really, really hard that I knew it would work."

"You had me fooled," Ellie said supportively, and Kit seemed pleased—but still pretty unhappy about the whole situation. Ellie sighed. "I thought starting small was the way to go. It's just one tiny little hammer!"

"Maybe we looked at it the wrong way," Toby said, pausing to move a beetle away from the patio stone he was working on. "Maybe instead of starting small, we should have started big."

"You think we should teach her to use a

drill? Or an electric saw?" Ellie asked, wondering how she'd convince her dad to let her borrow the saw. It was a tool she usually got to use only when he was there to supervise.

"Or maybe we should teach her about a different part of engineering. Maybe she'd like the part where you draw up plans more," Kit suggested.

Toby shook his head. "That's not what I meant. I'm thinking that perhaps we should have started with something that will help her in a *big* way. She thought the hammer just wouldn't be useful, right? But maybe if you built something that would be a *big* help, she'd be excited about it and would want to help. It'd have to be something bigger than fixing cabinet doors and table legs, though."

"Maybe you could add lots of windows to her downstairs so it gets better light, and she can move her studio," Kit suggested.

Ellie looked at the back wall of the house. "I don't know. I think you need big tools to smash bricks. And I bet she won't let us make holes in the side of her house."

"She likes espresso," Toby said. "What if you made an espresso delivery system?"

Ellie thought on this. If she made some sort of lever—like a seesaw—in Mrs. Curran's foyer, she could perhaps put the espresso on one end. Mrs. Curran would have to toss something heavy on the other end, and then it would shoot the espresso up . . . Ellie whipped out her notebook and began drawing.

"Wouldn't espresso go everywhere, though?" Kit asked when she saw Ellie's sketch.

"Maybe she could put it in a little cup with a lid," Toby suggested.

"I don't think espresso goes in those kinds of cups," Kit said. "And besides, she'd still have

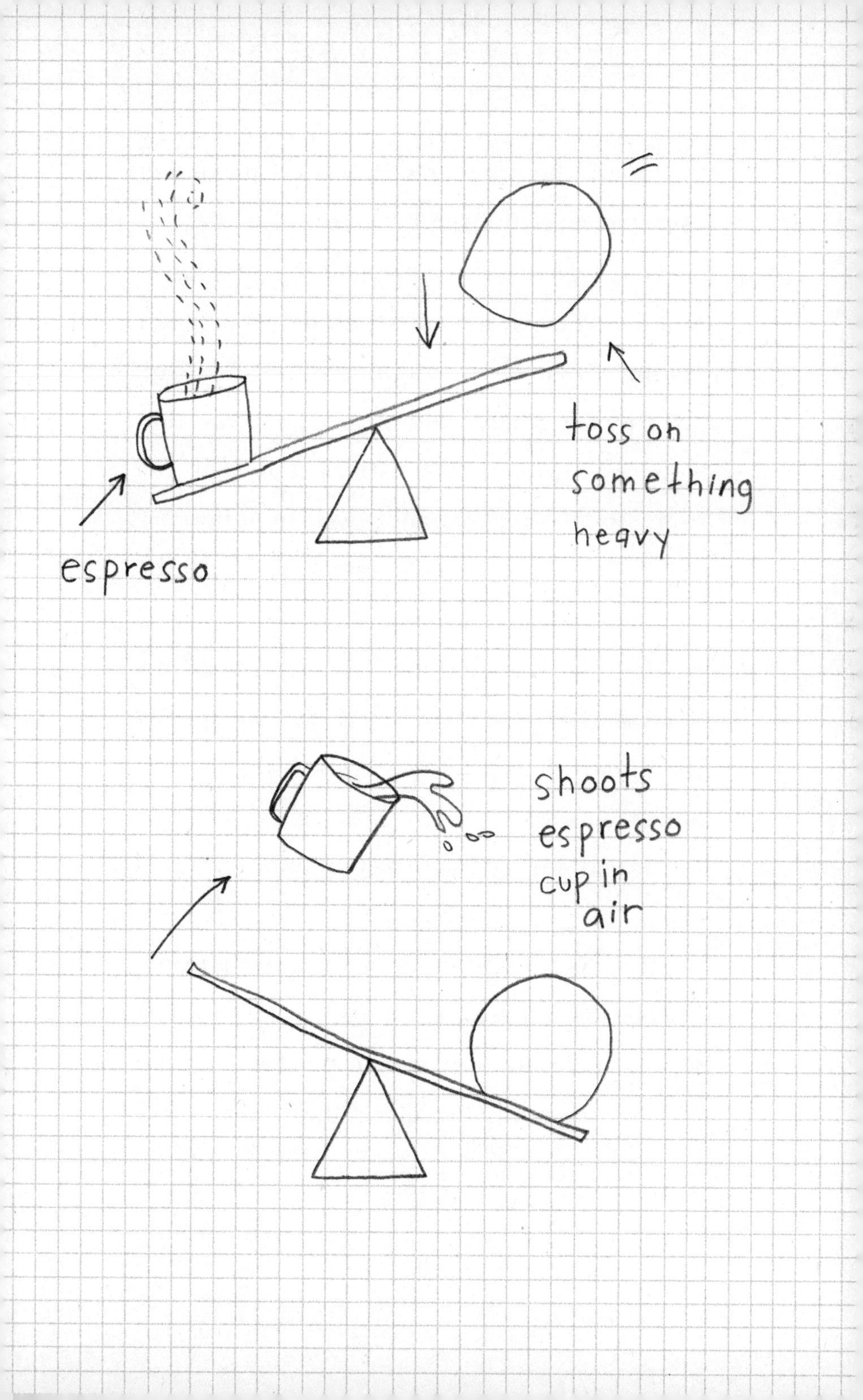
toss on
something
heavy
espresso
shoots
espresso
cup in
air

to go all the way downstairs to make her espresso, wouldn't she?"

Ellie sighed, which seemed to worry Toby and Kit—they weren't at all used to seeing her feeling down about engineering. Toby said, "Okay, okay, what if you put a giant straw that went all the way downstairs and sent the espresso *shooting up* to her studio and into her cup? Like an espresso *fountain*. Then she wouldn't have to leave her studio!"

"Oh, that's a good one," Kit said, nodding. "And maybe then you could put one in my room that sends milkshakes shooting upstairs and into a cup."

"I call an orange soda one!" Toby said excitedly.

"That is a really cool idea," Ellie said, thinking on how a machine like that would work. It would need lots of power to push a drink all the way upstairs, and then they'd need a way to keep it from just exploding all over the studio . . . Ellie frowned. "We only have one more day of coming to Mrs. Curran's. I think an espresso fountain will take us a lot longer to engineer and build. Plus, we probably ought to build it and test it somewhere that espresso won't get all over expensive dolls."

"I don't have anything that is too expensive to get covered in orange soda," Toby said hopefully.

Ellie went on without answering him. "What else would be a *big* help?" They all went quiet, thinking on this for a while. Every now and then one would open his or her mouth, then shut it and shake his or her head.

Until Ellie opened her mouth and left it open. Because . . . well. It was obvious!

"What is it, Ellie?" Kit asked.

"Ohhhhhhh," Ellie said. "*Eeeeeeeeee!*"

"Is she okay?" Toby asked Kit. "I saw a

television show where a boy started making noises like that, and it was because a ghost was in his brain."

"Ellie? Is there a ghost in your brain?" Kit asked, grabbing Ellie's hand.

"A ghost? Oh, no," Ellie said. "It's just–I know what we have to build! And it's just about as scary as a ghost in your brain."

"What?" Toby asked eagerly.

Ellie pressed her lips together, feeling a swirl of worried and excited. "We've got to build another elevator."

Chapter Ten

Ellie really did *like* rebuilding things and making them better. That was just part of engineering: you built something, tested it, and if it didn't work, you tinkered with it until it *did*.

But the elevator wasn't like most of her builds. For starters, it had been a capital-"D" Disaster: Kit's mom hadn't been able to get fancy replacement pickles in time, Ellie's dad had had to get special cream for all the bug bites he got while cleaning up glass, and the backyard *still* smelled like pickles (which was not a great smell in the middle of a hot summer day). The whole reason they were at Mrs. Curran's in the first place was because of how badly the elevator plan had gone!

It was pretty obvious, though, that a way to get heavy boxes upstairs to Mrs. Curran's studio was the perfect project. It would be such a big help to Mrs. Curran that she surely couldn't turn it down. Plus, they would really truly *need* Mrs. Curran's help to build it—they couldn't just start nailing things into her stair railings or hanging stuff from the foyer ceiling without her there.

"Here's what I'm thinking," Ellie told Kit and Toby that afternoon, in her workshop. She tore two pieces of paper from her notebook—one with the original elevator design and one with a new, improved, hopefully-not-capital-"D"-Disaster version. Ellie had been working on a new elevator design almost every night before bed, thinking on it during the day, and trying to trick her brain into dreaming about it while she slept. She was pretty sure she'd finally sorted out where her original design had gone wrong.

"Two of these?" Toby asked, pointing to the two pulleys on the new version.

Ellie nodded. "Yes. One pulley lets you lift something easier because you can *pull* instead of just heaving it up in your arms. But with *two* pulleys, it's like you're using two ropes instead of one, so you only have to work half as hard."

Kit's eyes widened. "What if you added even more pulleys?"

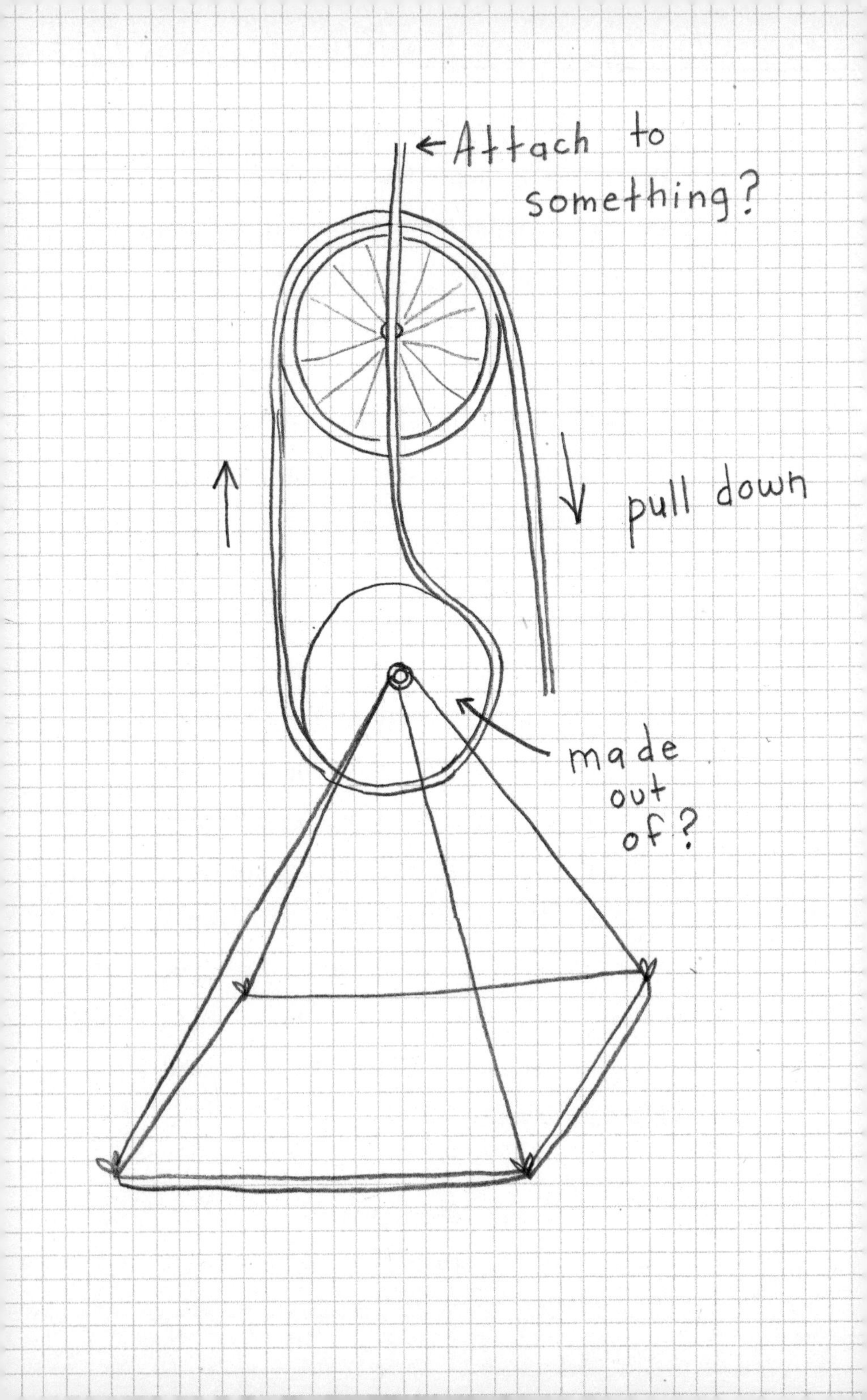
Attach to something?
pull down
made out of?

"That'd make it even easier, but I don't think there's time to make any more pulleys," Ellie said. "I thought we could put this hook here, too, so that it wraps up the rope and keeps the elevator from sliding back down to the ground. I think we should work on some bits of the elevator here, that way we don't have to start from scratch at Mrs. Curran's house."

"Good thinking. She probably wouldn't be very happy if we had to spread out all the nails and wood on her carpet in the foyer," Toby said.

"How do we keep everything from tipping off, like the pickles did?" Kit asked, studying the drawing.

Ellie pointed at the part of the drawing that showed the elevator platform. "When we did it last time, we had two ropes wrapped under this piece of table, so when the pickles sloshed, everything tipped. This time around, we'll use four ropes and tie them all up in the middle, see? So even if the boxes start to tip one way, the other ropes will stop them from totally sliding off."

"Let's not test it with anything in glass jars though, just in case," Kit said a little nervously. Ellie agreed.

They got to work on the new and improved elevator. Ellie used her drill—her very favorite tool—to drill holes on the other two edges of the tabletop. They threaded rope through those holes, and then Toby tied super-tight knots. Toby knew a lot about fancy knots, like the kinds sailors use, and was really excited to show Ellie and Kit all the different sorts he knew about.

"I think for the knots under the table, we ought to go with a figure-eight. It's a knot that lots of firefighters use," Toby said, nodding to himself.

"Sounds good," Ellie said, shrugging at Kit. "We'll need a place to connect the top pulley to the ceiling. Is there a light up there? Or maybe a plant hook? Or—"

"Oh! I know what to use!" Kit said, and hurriedly drew out a picture of Mrs. Curran's upstairs foyer on a piece of paper. Kit was a good artist—*and* she had a really good memory. She hadn't gotten a bad grade on a spelling test in basically her entire life, and she already knew her multiplication tables all the way into the twelves (Ellie was super stuck on the sixes). She handed her drawing of the foyer to Ellie, who drew the new and improved elevator over it. Ellie, Kit, and Toby looked at the drawing, then at the pieces they'd put together laid out on the workshop floor.

"It looks like it *should* work," Toby said.

"It looks like it *will* work," Kit said, patting Ellie's shoulder.

"It looks like it *has* to work," Ellie finished. "Mrs. Curran has to see that anyone can be an engineer. And besides, she has to find a good way to get those boxes upstairs. I don't want her to have to retire. No one should ever have to stop doing something they love to do."

Chapter Eleven

"Oh my," Mrs. Curran said when she opened the door the following morning. "What in the world is that?"

"An elevator!" Ellie said cheerfully. Kit and Toby were holding the tabletop behind her. The ropes were all hanging off it like spaghetti noodles. Ellie was holding two pulleys—one made out of the same tricycle wheel that the capital-"D" Disaster elevator was made out of, and a second one she'd made the night before out of two mini pizza pans she'd glued together.

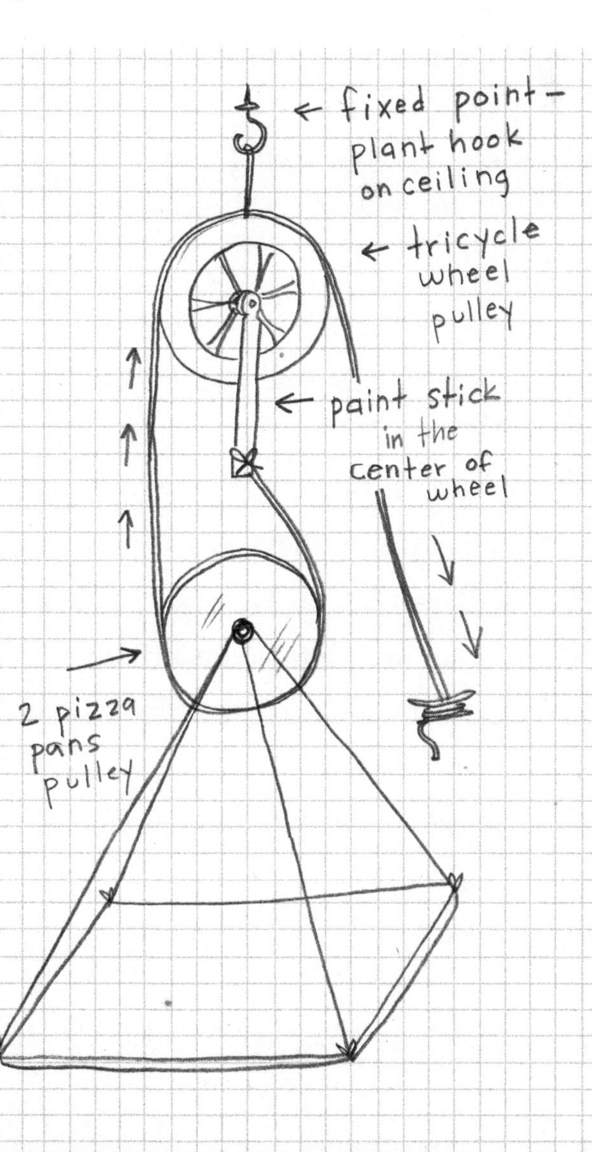

"Are you very sure you know what an elevator is, dear?" Mrs. Curran asked, setting her espresso cup down on a table in the foyer.

"Yes," Ellie said confidently. "We made it for *you*, Mrs. Curran."

Mrs. Curran's eyes widened and Ellie could see just how neatly she'd put on her eye makeup. "How . . . erm . . . kind."

"Getting pretty heavy back here," Toby said, and shifted so that he could hold the tabletop better.

"Excuse us," Ellie said politely, and scooted past Mrs. Curran. Toby and Kit followed behind her, and Mrs. Curran had to step out of the way to allow the tabletop through. Toby and Kit set it down gently on the foyer rug. Mrs. Curran shut the door, but then looked out the side window, like she thought she might need to flag down someone for help.

"I'm not quite sure I understand what is happening here," Mrs. Curran said, clasping her hands together.

"Remember how I told you that I'm an engineer?" Ellie asked. Mrs. Curran's eyes flicked over to Toby, like when she heard the word "engineer" she thought of him, but Ellie didn't let herself get upset. She kept going. "I designed an elevator for you to get the boxes of doll supplies from your garage to your studio. Toby and Kit helped."

"Oh my," Mrs. Curran said for the second time in only a few minutes.

"We can put it together and show you how it works, but we need your help," Ellie finished, putting her hands on her hips just above her tool belt.

Mrs. Curran was smiling in a tight way. "That's a very sweet offer, but—"

"Mrs. Curran, didn't the dolly work great?

You said it was very clever," Toby reminded her. "That was Ellie's design."

"And you thought all the fixing we did in the house was great enough that you gave us all presents. That was Ellie's work, too," Kit said.

"Yes, yes, that was all quite nice, but elevators are much more elaborate, aren't they?" Mrs. Curran said. "I think perhaps this is the sort of thing better left to more experienced engineers."

"We already have experience building elevators," Ellie said insistently, leaving out the fact that their experience was really just building a single, terrible elevator. "Plus, you're going to help us! You're an experienced *person*, and I'm an engineer, so together we're the same as an experienced engineer."

"That doesn't really make sense," Kit whispered. Ellie shushed her. This wasn't a time for making sense—this was a time for getting things done.

"I don't know if I can be much help," Mrs. Curran said, looking worried.

"Sure you can! And just think, Mrs. Curran: once we're done, you'll be able to move the boxes of supplies upstairs on your own, to your studio. Think about how great that will be! It'll solve such a big problem, and you won't have to worry anymore about needing to give up painting dolls," Kit said, stepping closer and giving her best pageant smile (Ellie knew it well, since she usually went to Kit's pageants to cheer her on).

"Ahhhh," Mrs. Curran said, cringing—but the kind of cringing that Ellie knew meant she was considering this. "I suppose the other things that Toby—er, that *Ellie*—did were quite helpful. All right. Go ahead."

The three of them cheered, and it sounded for a minute like Mrs. Curran was cheering with them, but then it turned out she was just making worried noises deep in her throat.

Mrs. Curran got herself another espresso and sat down in a fluffy chair in the foyer. Kit dashed up the stairs and studied the pull-down attic door—this is what she'd remembered and drawn for the others yesterday. She opened it just a crack, then slipped a rope around the door. It was the perfect place to mount the top pulley!

In the meantime, Ellie worked on the bottom pizza-pan pulley. "Here, Mrs. Curran," she said, and brought the pulley over to Mrs. Curran's chair. "Could you put this rope through the pulley?"

"Hm?" Mrs. Curran said. "Me? Is this a pastry tray?"

"Yes," Ellie said, "and yes again—well, if pizzas are pastries, it is." Ellie went on, "See, the rope will slide in between the edges where the pans meet, and that will help lift the tabletop."

“How clever,” Mrs. Curran said, pinching her brows together. She took the rope from Ellie’s hands and slid it through the pulley. “There you go.”

“Perfect,” Ellie said, and hurried to put the pulley in place. She lifted up the ropes on the tabletop next, then took her tape measure from her pocket. “Here, I need help with this, too,” she said.

“What should I do?” Mrs. Curran asked, looking a little wary but a little bit curious, too. “A little bit curious” was a big improvement, and it gave Ellie hope.

“I need to measure these ropes to be sure they’re all the same length—otherwise the tabletop might be crooked, and things could slide off it. I’ll hold the rope tight, and you slide the tape measure out to tell me how long the rope is,” Ellie said, and handed Mrs. Curran the tape measure. Mrs. Curran turned it over in her palm a few times, like it was something particularly magical, then pulled the measuring bit out. She held it up to the first of the ropes and, after a few moments of squinting, called out how long it was. She went a bit quicker with the second rope, and by the time they were measuring the last one, she was using the tape measure like a pro.

"This one is a bit longer," she said. "Four little lines on this tape measure longer."

"That's one fourth of an inch," Ellie said, then held her finger and thumb a teeny bit apart. "About this much! But that little bit makes a big difference in engineering, so we need to trim it shorter."

"I can get some scissors!" Mrs. Curran said, and now she sounded really *truly* excited. Kit grinned and gave Ellie a thumbs-up sign as Mrs. Curran zipped to the kitchen in her high heels to fetch the scissors. By the time she got back, they had nearly everything ready to go.

They tied the ropes to the one on the pulley. Ellie duct-taped the hook where the rope would wrap up to the bottom of the stair banister. (She went with duct tape because she wasn't sure how Mrs. Curran would feel about her using screws and her drill on the banister.)

"Is it ready?" Mrs. Curran asked eagerly, looking at the ropes that ran from the foyer floor up, through the stairwell, to the second story of the house.

"Yes! Well, almost—we need to test it first," Ellie said. She looked around the room and saw the pillow on the chair Mrs. Curran had been sitting on. "Let's use the pillow—that way, if it doesn't work, nothing will get broken."

"I can't believe we didn't think of that with the first elevator," Toby said.

"What was that?" Mrs. Curran asked.

"Nothing!" Toby said. "Never mind me! There was just a ghost in my brain."

Mrs. Curran frowned and was about to ask

another question, but Ellie stepped in. "So, Mrs. Curran—the two pulleys make the boxes weigh half as much as they normally would. Just pull this rope and wrap it up on the hook as you go, and it'll slowly lift the elevator. *Way* easier than carrying the box up the steps, right?"

Mrs. Curran's eyes were glittery. "Oh, I do hope this works! You know, it never once occurred to me to have someone build an elevator."

"You *helped* build it, Mrs. Curran! You're an engineer too, now. Anyone can be an engineer—girls and boys and doll painters," Ellie said very seriously, because this was the thing she wanted Mrs. Curran to understand more than anything else.

"Oh! An engineer! Me!" Mrs. Curran said, and she still sounded like this was something very funny instead of something very true.

Ellie was a little discouraged—but perhaps seeing the elevator in action would change Mrs. Curran's mind.

"Come on! Come take a look at the whole thing from the top!" Ellie said, and bounded upstairs. Mrs. Curran followed behind. She was, as always, wearing her high heels, but she was moving much faster than normal—she was hurrying up the steps, gripping the handrail tightly. Seeing her so eager to see the elevator made Ellie's heart feel like a bouncy ball in her chest.

Until the accident happened.

Chapter Twelve

First Mrs. Curran lifted her foot to climb the next stair—totally normal. But she put her foot down a little bit sideways. And then her foot twisted in a way that was very *not* normal. Mrs. Curran grabbed hold of the railing to keep from falling, but she cried out and still slipped a little. Her ankle bent to the step and her arm yanked against the railing and her left high-heel shoe went tumbling down the steps.

Ellie yelped. Kit squealed. Toby covered his eyes.

But then Ellie realized that yelping wasn't going to help a single bit, so she dashed toward Mrs. Curran and grabbed hold of her arm, just in case she was going to tumble down the steps just like her shoe had. "Are you all right?" Ellie asked frantically.

"Oh, dear, yes—*oh!*" Mrs. Curran said. Her voice was shaky and her face was all scrunched up. Something was hurting her, *bad*. "I lost my footing."

"I've got it!" Toby said, holding up her lost shoe. He bounded up the steps and offered the shoe to Mrs. Curran, but she didn't take it, because her eyes were shut tight. Kit had joined them now, and the three of them stood on the stairs around Mrs. Curran, waiting for her to tell them what to do. She was the grown-up, after all—when things got serious, grown-ups were supposed to have the answers.

"Would you like some ice, Mrs. Curran?" Ellie suggested—that's what the gym teacher gave her once when she jammed her finger playing dodgeball.

"No, no." Mrs. Curran winced. "I think I just need a minute."

"I can make a tourniquet," Toby said. "But those are more for when you're bleeding or have snakebites."

"I can get some Band-Aids," Kit suggested.

Mrs. Curran didn't answer. Ellie was starting to think this situation called for more than Band-Aids or tourniquets, which meant it was worse than bleeding or snakebites. Ellie didn't have any experience with snakebites, but she knew they were no kind of good.

"I think we need to call my parents for

help," Ellie said firmly. "Kit, Toby, you sit with Mrs. Curran, okay?" They nodded, and Ellie hurried to the phone and called her house. Her dad answered, and within a few minutes, he and Ellie's mom had arrived. They decided to call for an ambulance, but Ellie felt a lot better once Mrs. Curran had been taken to the hospital—it was, after all, full of grown-ups who had answers.

While they waited for Ellie's mom and dad to talk to the people in the ambulance, Ellie, Kit, and Toby stood in the foyer, staring at the elevator platform.

"Is it our fault?" Kit asked quietly, almost in a whisper.

"I don't know. I don't think so. But it feels like it is," Ellie answered, fiddling with the tops of the tools in her belt (that's what she did when she was nervous).

They stopped talking when Ellie's parents

came back inside. The ambulance was driving away, but it didn't have lights or sirens on. This seemed like a good thing to Ellie; they must not be in a big hurry, which must mean Mrs. Curran was mostly okay.

Ellie's mom knelt down beside the three of them, so she was eye level. She smiled, which she normally didn't do when Ellie interrupted her workday, and in a lot of ways, that made Ellie even more scared, because it was so not normal.

"Don't worry," Ellie's mom said. She could tell how worried Ellie was—she was good at knowing what Ellie was feeling. "You three did the exact right thing, calling us. Mrs. Curran is going to be just fine. She just twisted her ankle a bit, I think. It's always a good idea, though, to call for a doctor when an older person has a fall."

"Do *you* think it's our fault?" Kit asked Ellie's mom.

Ellie's mom shook her head quickly. "Not a single bit!"

"But she was hurrying upstairs to try out the new elevator," Ellie said, pointing. Ellie's parents both looked over to where Ellie was pointing. They grimaced at the exact same time.

"You built *another* elevator? *Indoors?*" Ellie's mom asked.

"We improved the design," Ellie said.

"I can see that," Ellie's dad said, looking impressed. He walked over to the elevator and inspected the pulley on the floor. "Very clever—oh, and look! A wheel to pull the platform up! Wait, are those my little pizza pans?"

"We were showing Mrs. Curran that anyone can be an engineer," Ellie said glumly. "She helped us with it. It was going so great!"

"Accidents happen. But, just like the other elevator, this is a good reminder that you need to be careful when building things," Ellie's dad said, then shivered a little. He didn't need to say it out loud for Ellie to know he was remembering all those pickles.

Ellie also knew what her dad meant—that it was important to be careful and not get carried away and rush. But . . . she couldn't help feeling that what he was really saying was this elevator was *also* a capital-"D" Disaster.

Chapter Thirteen

"I was thinking that perhaps tomorrow, we can go visit Mrs. Curran at the hospital," Ellie's dad said at dinner that evening. They were eating macaroni with broccoli in it, which Ellie thought was a really sneaky way of making her eat broccoli since it was totally impossible to separate the macaroni from the broccoli.

"I'm not sure that's a good idea," Ellie said, staring at her macaroni-with-broccoli.

Ellie's mom frowned. "Why's that?"

Ellie sighed and pushed a lump of broccoli under some noodles. "I'm scared."

"Scared?" Ellie's dad said, eyebrows lifting up so they almost touched his hair. "That's not like you, Ellie."

Ellie didn't say anything, but neither did her parents, which usually meant they were waiting for her to talk again. Finally, she did. "What if Mrs. Curran is mad at me because she got hurt?"

"I don't think she is. It was an accident."

"So were the pickles, but Kit's mom was super mad."

"Ah," Ellie's mom and dad said at almost the same time, like they'd just solved something. Her dad went on. "Ellie, sometimes things go wrong when you're engineering—just like how sometimes things go wrong when you're drawing or singing or even just walking."

"It's true," Ellie's mom said. "You know how often I trip!"

She did trip an awful lot. "But that's not the same as things going wrong when you're engineering," Ellie said. "If you trip, you only hurt yourself. If you mess up when you're engineering, you hurt twenty-four jars of pickles and Toby gets in trouble and Kit's mom hates your shelephant saddle and Mrs. Curran gets hurt."

"Those are all very different situations," Ellie's mom said.

"And you'll remember that the reason you got in trouble with the pickle situation is because you were rushing instead of being careful, and you took things without permission."

"That's why Toby got in trouble too," Ellie said, nodding.

"Is that why Kit's mom hated the–what was it, a sheepephant saddle?" her dad asked.

“Shelephant. And no, I think all the legs on it just freaked her out,” Ellie answered, sighing.

Ellie’s parents seemed to decide at once not to ask any more questions about the saddle. Her dad said, “Engineering is supposed to *help* people, Ellie, right? Mrs. Curran’s fall was an accident, and from the looks of things, you were trying very hard to help her. I think that new elevator looked top-notch.”

Ellie smiled a little. She couldn’t help it. Her dad said things were “top-notch” only when he really meant it, after all.

“Mrs. Curran must have been terribly excited about your elevator, to try to run up the stairs and to let you build it right there in her foyer. It sounds like you really proved to her that you—that *anyone*—can be an engineer. So I bet she would be really happy for you to go visit her,” Ellie’s mom said.

"Okay," Ellie said, trying to smush down all the old scared feelings underneath the new glow-y feelings in her chest.

"Maybe we can bring her something nice. Does she like candies?" Ellie's dad asked.

"I don't think so. Mostly she likes espresso. And hummus! We could take her some hummus, if you know where to buy some," Ellie said.

Ellie's mom and dad looked at each other again.

"I didn't think people her age liked espresso *or* hummus," Ellie's dad mused, shaking his head.

Ellie gave him a serious look. "You're making *assumptions*, Dad. Espresso is for all types of people. So is hummus. There's no such thing as old-people stuff and young-people stuff, only stuff." She didn't tell him that she had made lots of assumptions about Mrs. Curran in the beginning too—like that she would make cookies or need a lotion squeezer.

Ellie's dad laughed a little bit. "You're right. We'll go first thing in the morning, then, and we'll pick up some espresso and hummus on the way. Sound good?"

"Sounds perfect."

Chapter Fourteen

Ellie had only been to the hospital a few times in her entire life—once to visit Kit when she got her tonsils taken out, once when her aunt got really sick for a long time, and once when her dad *thought* Ellie had broken her arm, but it turned out she hadn't. Ellie was glad she hadn't but was sort of sad she didn't get a cast for everyone in Mrs. Funderburk's class to sign. She had already decided on a pink cast, and if they didn't have pink, purple.

Each time, she went to a totally different part of the hospital. To visit Mrs. Curran, they went to a section where the halls were painted oatmeal brown and the floors were mint green. She wondered why they didn't put cartoon characters on the walls here or have games in the waiting room, since those were her favorite things in the part she'd visited not to get a cast. Even grandma-age people like Mrs. Curran probably liked cartoons and games when they were sick, didn't they?

Ellie's dad talked to a man dressed all in blue at a desk, and they walked down the hall to room 503. Her dad balanced the espresso cup on the container of hummus in his right hand. Ellie was holding the pita chips they'd gotten to go with the hummus—she hoped she'd chosen the right kind of both. Her dad made sure the espresso was steady, then knocked on the door.

Ellie's stomach squiggled when Mrs. Curran's voice said, "Come in! I'm decent!" from the other side. Her knees locked up and her feet glued down.

"Ellie?" her dad said.

"Hmm?"

"You have to open the door to go in. That's how doors work," her dad said in a firm voice.

Ellie ran her fingers across her tool belt. What if Mrs. Curran had decided everything was Ellie's fault after all? What if she yelled at Ellie because now she was stuck in the section of the hospital with no cartoons or games or dolls to paint? Ellie wished she'd brought a doll—though, Mrs. Curran would probably have wanted one of *her* dolls to work on, and she'd have had to get back into Mrs. Curran's house, but maybe if they went *right now—*

"Hey now—are you Ellie, Engineer, or Ellie, Scared?" her dad asked.

"Engineer. Definitely engineer," Ellie said as firmly as she could, and turned the knob.

Mrs. Curran's room was sunny, and there were big pink and white flowers on her bedside table. She looked . . . exactly the way she always looked. Her makeup was flawless! Her hair was curled. She wasn't wearing her high heels, but there was a pair by the bed that someone must have brought for her. She was sitting up straight in her hospital bed, and if Ellie squinted so that the little machines and charts and hospital walls blurred away, she could pretend Mrs. Curran was sitting at her studio desk.

"You look great!" Ellie said loudly. "You don't look sick at all!"

"Well, I'm not sick—I'm just a little delicate on my feet," Mrs. Curran said, and smiled. "Oh! Is that an espresso?"

"We brought you that and some hummus. Ellie chose them," Ellie's dad said, sounding a little wary—but Mrs. Curran looked delighted and reached for both. She opened up the pita chips and laid them out on the table, offering Ellie them and the hummus.

"Oh, no thank you," Ellie said politely. It still looked like mud in a bowl, in her opinion.

"I'm going to step outside and return some calls, okay?" Ellie's dad said, and smiled at her in a way that made her pretty certain he was actually going to go play games on his phone—he just wanted Ellie to have some time to talk to Mrs. Curran alone. She gave him a thumbs-up, and he ducked out. Ellie's stomach was still a little squiggly. She sat down in a pink chair with metal arms and swung her legs back and forth.

“I’m glad you’re okay, Mrs. Curran. We were really worried,” she said in a low voice.

“I was worried too there, for a moment. You and your friends were perfect though—you called for help, and I’ll be right as rain in no time.” Mrs. Curran paused, swallowed the chip she was eating, then went on in a more serious voice, “There is one thing I’m rather upset about, though—that elevator.”

Ellie’s teeth mashed together, and she held her breath. Her stomach went from squiggly to hurricane-y.

“That was quite an ambitious project, wasn’t it, for someone who isn’t always very cautious when she gets excited?” Mrs. Curran said sternly.

“Yes, Mrs. Curran,” Ellie said in a tiny voice. She swung her legs back and forth even harder.

“And it was an ambitious project for

someone who hasn't built a working elevator before."

Ellie nodded glumly.

"*And* for someone who isn't an engineer."

Ellie's eyes sprang up—she couldn't just nod at this! Her voice went high and loud and sad, and she shook her head frantically. "No! Mrs. Curran, I *am* an engineer! Anyone can be an engineer!"

Mrs. Curran looked alarmed, and Ellie couldn't blame her—she was practically shouting at an adult (not *angry* shouting, but shouting all the same). She smiled a little. "Ellie Bell, don't be ridiculous. I wasn't talking about you. I was talking about me! I got too excited and hurried up the steps, and I haven't built an elevator, and I certainly am no engineer."

Ellie blinked. "You were excited about the elevator?"

Mrs. Curran rolled her eyes. Ellie had never

seen a grandma-age person roll her eyes, but then again, Mrs. Curran wasn't like most grandma-age people. "Of course I was! Something that helped me get the doll supplies upstairs? Why wouldn't I be excited! And what's more, I've never so much as built a birdhouse before—I never dreamed I would be able to help build an elevator."

Ellie grinned, though she was also still hurricane-y, and also her eyes were a little watery, because there were all sorts of feelings *kapow*ing into one another in her chest. "So—you *do* know that I'm an engineer? That anyone can be an engineer?"

"Well, I certainly do now. How could I deny it, after seeing you in action? I have to admit, I thought it must be Toby behind all the building at first," Mrs. Curran said carefully. "I've just never met a little girl who loves engineering before you."

"I really do love it, Mrs. Curran. Toby likes engineering fine, but not the way I do. Though he *does* really like playing with dolls," Ellie said.

"Oh!" Mrs. Curran said, looking surprised and pleased. "Well, I should have given him one then! I just thought that ant farm looked so interesting! They're clever creatures, you know. I would have loved to get that as a gift."

"You know, you could get yourself an ant farm, Mrs. Curran," Ellie said, lifting her eyebrows, still grinning. "Ant farms aren't only for boys—just like engineering."

Mrs. Curran laughed, then sipped on her espresso. "You have a very good point, Ellie Bell. Perhaps he'll trade me that ant farm for a doll of his own. And speaking of engineering—I see you have your tool belt with you. I wondered if you might help me with something."

"Of course! With what?" Ellie asked, immediately looking around the room, making a list in her brain of all the potential building materials. There weren't many, because just about everything in there looked like it was Very Important. But she was pretty sure she could take apart the chairs and put them back together again, easy-peasy, so those could be useful . . .

"The doctor says I ought to use crutches for a few weeks just to play it safe. And I thought, goodness, what a pain in the rear! It's hard to carry much of anything when you've got crutches . . . unless . . . someone were to design some new, improved, *better* crutches and teach me how to build them."

Ellie's eyes lit up, and she clapped her hands together. "Absolutely! Oh, Mrs. Curran,

I have some really good ideas!" She grabbed her notepad and bounced up onto the side of the bed so Mrs. Curran could see, then started to draw her—*their*—next build: Project 67: World's Best Crutches.

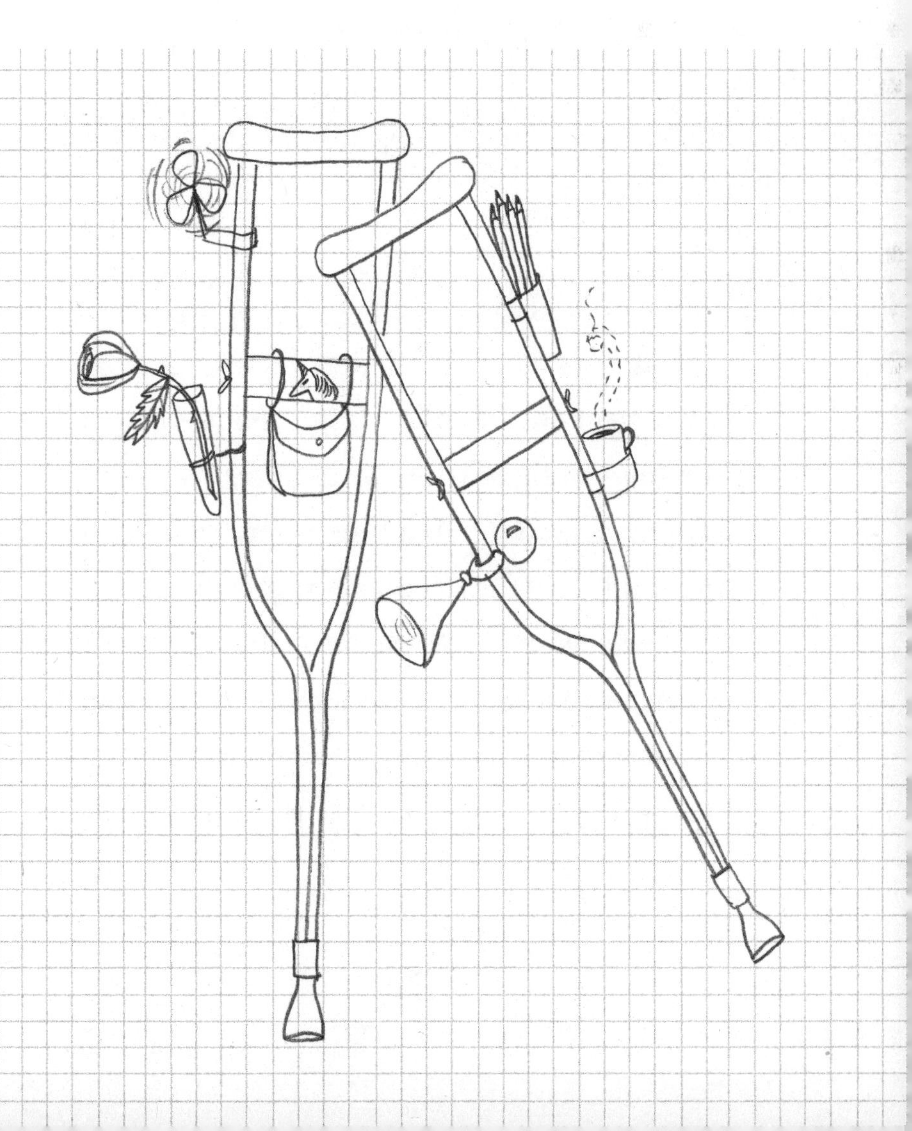

Chapter Fifteen

"Is everyone ready?" Ellie shouted from the top of the stairs at Mrs. Curran's house. Mrs. Curran was standing beside her with the crutches they'd made together tucked under her arm. Toby was positioned halfway up the stairs; Kit was at the bottom with the elevator platform, which they'd piled high with pillows. Ellie's dad was standing in the doorway to the kitchen with his arms crossed over his chest, watching carefully and looking very pleased.

"Ready!" Kit said, bouncing up and down.

"We're a go!" Toby shouted louder than he needed to, in a very official voice.

"Let's do it," Mrs. Curran said, smiling. "Would you like to do the honors, Ellie?"

"No way, Mrs. Curran. It's your elevator," Ellie answered.

Mrs. Curran smiled even harder, then shuffled over to the banister where the elevator wheel was. She steadied herself and then began to turn the handle slowly. Ellie held her breath as she watched.

The rope between the two pulleys tightened; the rope pieces attached to the elevator platform straightened out. And then . . . it began to lift off the ground! It inched up as Mrs. Curran turned the wheel, with the pillows perfectly balanced. Nothing tipped or fell or crashed! It was working, and it was working *perfectly*!

"You're doing it, Mrs. Curran! It looks great!" Toby called, jumping up and down on the steps.

"Almost there!" Kit yelled.

Mrs. Curran's eyes were wide and happy and excited as she turned the wheel the last few times, until the elevator was level with the stair banister. Then, she released the wheel, threw her hands into the air, and wrapped her arms tightly around Ellie. Ellie smooshed her back hard.

"Look at that! You're a brilliant engineer, Ellie!" Mrs. Curran said over the sound of everyone cheering.

Ellie beamed. "You're an engineer now too, Mrs. Curran! How does it feel?"

"It's very . . ." Mrs. Curran took a deep

breath and smiled when she said, "*Unexpected.* I'm so glad I won't have to wait for someone to help me get my supplies upstairs. Which, speaking of supplies—Toby? I have a business proposition for you."

Toby darted upstairs. Mrs. Curran walked (well, *crutched*, but she was moving quite well and speedily) into her studio and emerged with a doll. It was exactly like the ones she'd given Ellie and Kit—except for one thing. This one was wearing a *tool belt.* Ellie's eyes went wide. A doll with a tool belt! It didn't have any tools in it, but *still.* Toby was the luckiest person in the world.

"Would you be interested in trading in the ant farm I gave you for this doll? I heard you might prefer her to the ants."

"Yes! Yes, please!" Toby said, reaching for the doll and looking a bit overwhelmed.

"A tool belt? That's so cool!" Kit said

when she arrived and saw the doll in Toby's hands.

"I thought so, too," Mrs. Curran said. "Which is why . . ." She paused for a minute to reach into her pockets, and a moment later was holding two more doll tool belts. She dropped one each into Kit's and Ellie's hands. "I made them for you myself! But I'm afraid I don't know enough about tools yet to make those. I was hoping that you three might come over and help me learn?"

Ellie felt like she might *explode* with excitement–a working elevator, a tool belt for her doll, and an ant farm for Mrs. Curran. "Absolutely!" she said. Toby and Kit nodded.

"Wonderful," Mrs. Curran answered. "Now, if everyone would like to head downstairs, I have some snacks in the fridge. It'll take me a moment to get down there . . . unless . . . I take the elevator . . ."

Everyone froze.

"Um, Mrs. Curran, the elevator works, but I don't know if a person should get on it . . . ," Ellie began.

Mrs. Curran laughed and poked Ellie in the ribs. "Just kidding! Come on, let's take the stairs. For now."

ELLIE BELL'S GUIDE TO MACHINES

(THE SIMPLE ONES, ANYWAY)

Pulley

Pulleys might be simple, but they are so *so* useful—they pull up little things, like the blinds in your house, and the heavy things, like stuff on construction cranes. The reason they make it easier to move stuff is because they let you work *with* gravity instead of against it. So, let's say you need to get something heavy, like a box of coloring books, up onto your playset. You *could* just carry them up in your arms, but that would be really hard and you might fall down. You could also just tie a rope around them, climb to the top of your playset, and then pull them up, but that'd be really hard too. But if you put a pulley up at the top of your playset, you'd be able to stand on the ground and lift the coloring books by pulling straight down on the rope. If you wanted to make it even *easier*, you could add more pulleys, because the more you've got, the easier it is to lift something!

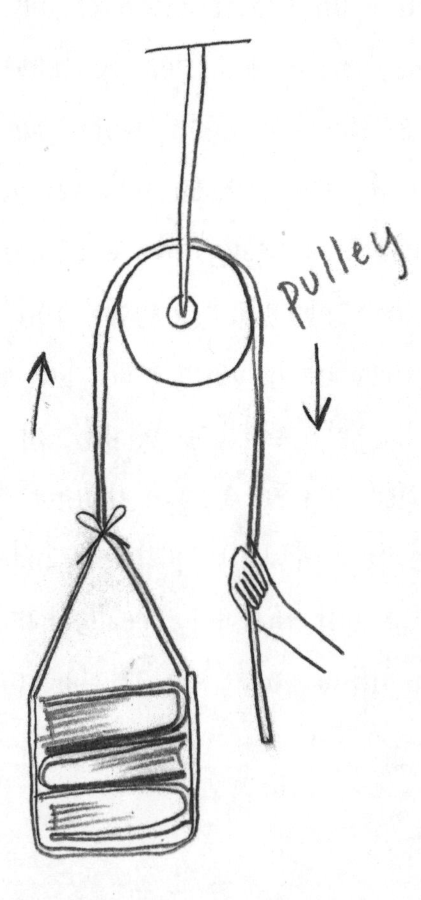

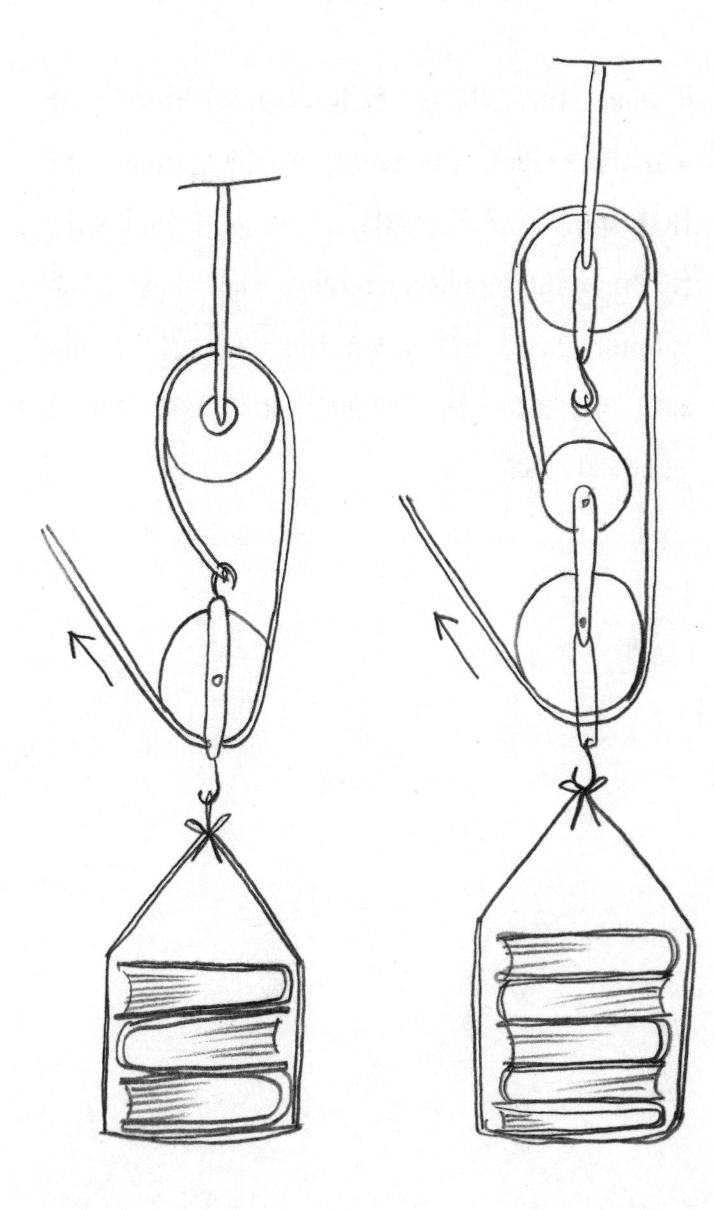

Wheel and Axle

A wheel and axle is really two machines that work together. The wheel is the round part that spins, and the axle is the part that goes through the middle and keeps the wheel from spinning right off down the road. It's really easy to see the wheel and axle on a wheelbarrow:

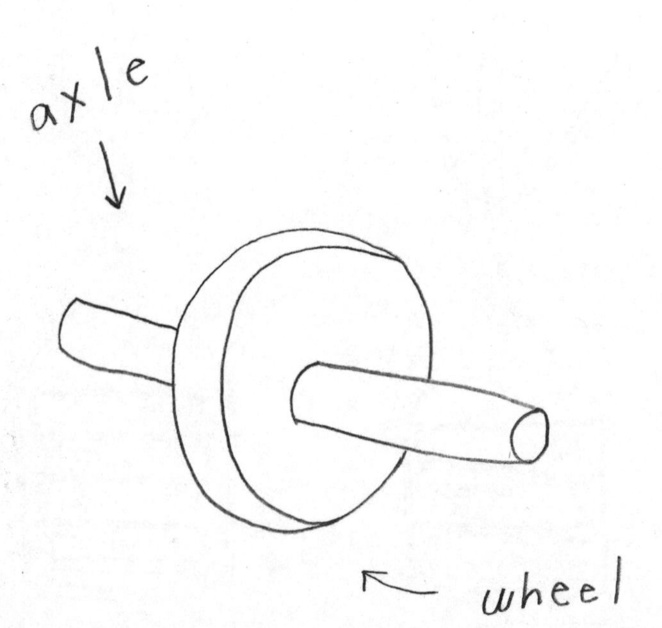

There are more wheels and axles than you might have realized. A rolling pin, for example, is a wheel and axle! So are the pencil sharpeners with the cranks that you might have in your school. And don't forget Ferris wheels! They're maybe my favorite wheel and axle of all.

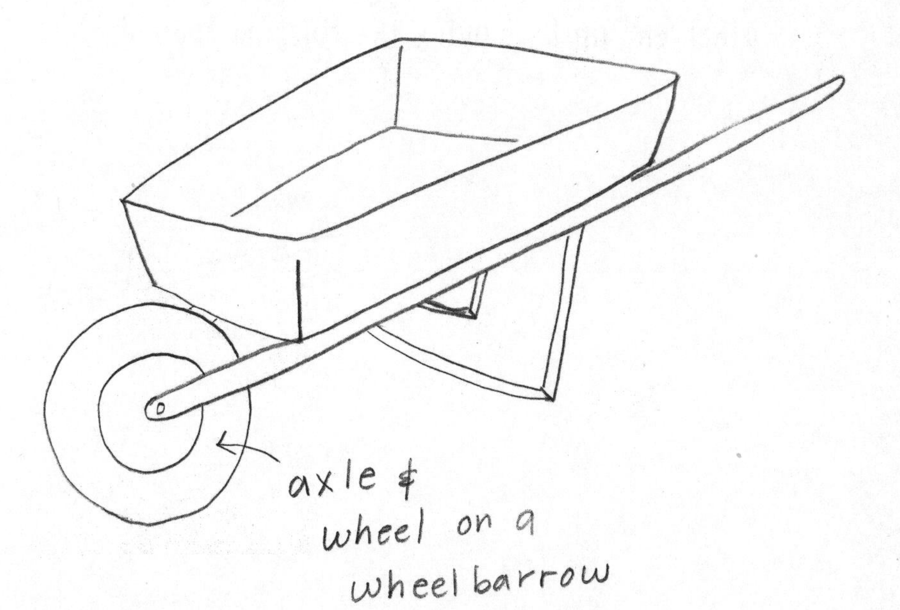

Lever

Levers are *everywhere*, even if you don't realize it! Seesaws are great examples of a lever—there's something on both ends of the plank, and then the little bit in the middle that the plank rests on, which is called the *fulcrum*. When you push one end of a seesaw down, the other end lifts up! You can really change how easy or hard it is to lift the other end up by moving the fulcrum around:

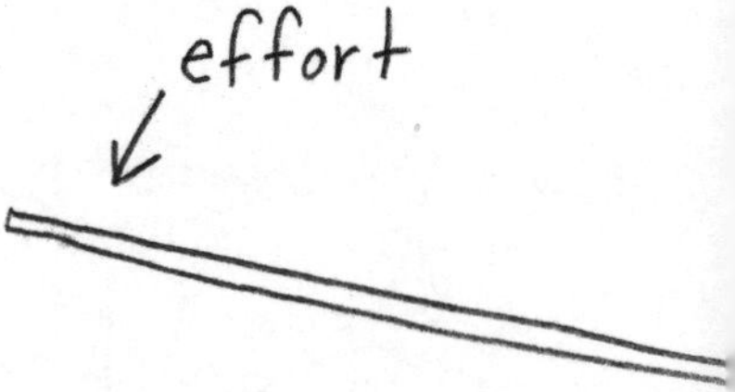

effort

Seesaws aren't the only types of levers though. The handle on the toilet flush-er is a lever, staplers are a type of lever . . . even forks are levers—your elbow is the fulcrum!

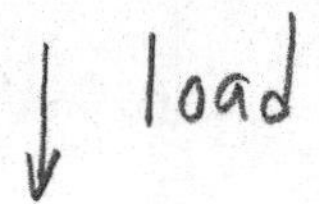

Wedge

A wedge is an extra-super-simple machine. Wedges are mostly just blades that help push things apart—like the sharp bit of an axe, or a nail, or even your teeth. If your ears are pierced, even your earrings are teeny tiny wedges!

Also, you might not want to tell *everyone* this, but you know how sometimes you get *wedgies* (it's okay—we all get them sometimes)? Well, in that case, your underpants are the wedge! Simple machines really are *everywhere*.

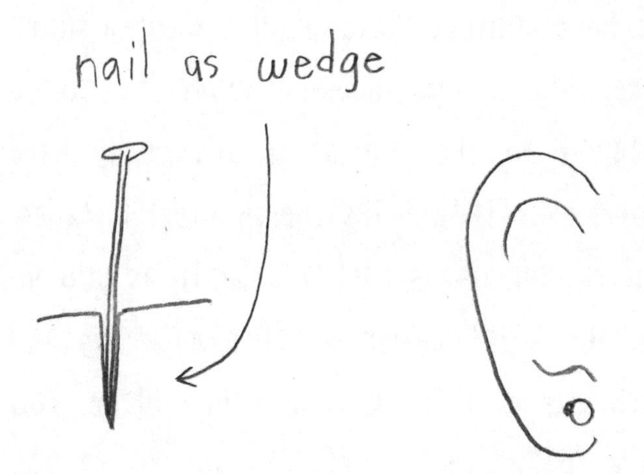

Incline Plane

If you have ever in your whole life gone up or down stairs or a ramp or a hill, then you've used an incline plane. Incline planes go from one level to another at an angle. The steeper the angle, the harder it is to move up the incline plane—but the shallower the angle, the longer the incline plane has to be. Have you ever taken your bike up a super steep hill in your neighborhood? If you go straight to the top of it, it's really hard work, even though it's the shortest distance. But if you zigzag back and forth as you go up, it's a lot easier, because each *zig* and each *zag* is a teeny tiny incline plane. You have to be extra careful to not zig or zag if a car is coming though.

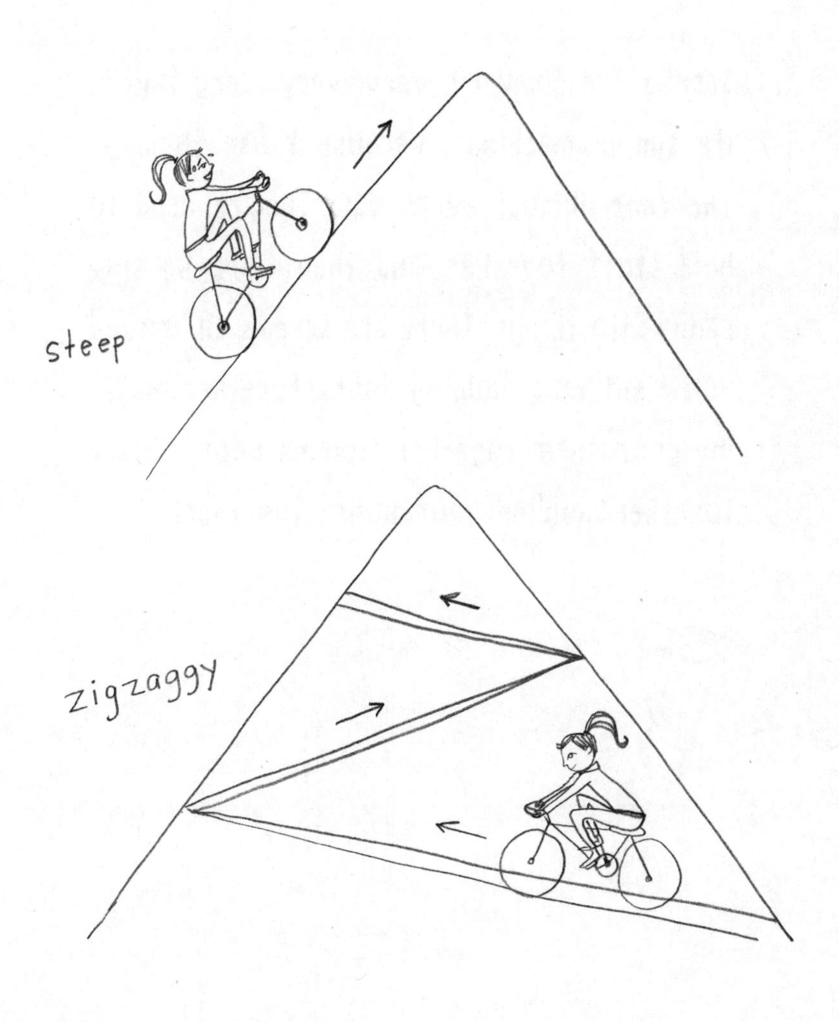
steep
zigzaggy

Screw

Screws are my very, very, very, very favorite simple machines, because I use them *all the time*. Almost every day! They're used to hold stuff together, and they work by spiraling into things. There are screws all around you right now: holding doors together, holding your chair together, holding your glasses together, holding your house together!

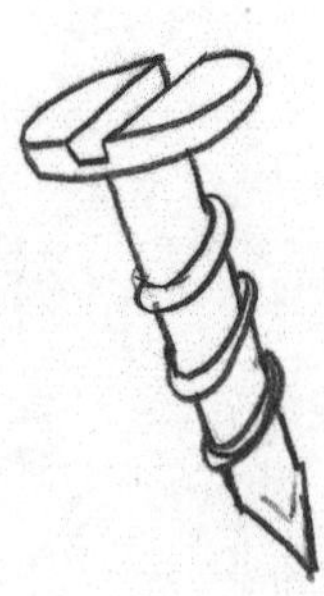

If you really think about it, a screw is an incline plane and a wedge smashed together: the sharp top is a wedge, and the spiral bit is an incline plane that goes round and round and round into stuff.

What will be Ellie's next fantastic engineering project?

Read on for a sneak peek to find out!

Ellie Bell was standing at the very, very edge, looking over.

It wasn't a terribly high edge, but it was *not* something she wanted to fall off. It was definitely not something she wanted to *skateboard* off, even though she'd designed and built it for exactly that purpose—Project 71: Fold-up! Light-up! Skateboard Ramp!

(She put lots of exclamation points in this project title, since she felt like it was extra exciting.)

Ellie wasn't the skateboarder, though—Kit was. And Kit looked *very* ready to skateboard right off the edge, down the ramp, then up the other side.

"Here goes!" Kit said excitedly, rapping on her bright-pink helmet to make sure it was in place. Kit's skateboard was pink, too, except for the purple otters she'd drawn on the underside, and so were her kneepads and wrist guards. Kit liked pink basically as much as Ellie liked purple, which was a *lot*. Ellie held a rectangle-shaped battery in one hand and the end of the wire of string lights in the other. The lights went all around the edges of the ramp and down the middle. It was the first time she'd ever built something with lights on it before! Ellie wrapped the end of the wire around the little circle on the end of the battery, and the lights instantly lit up.

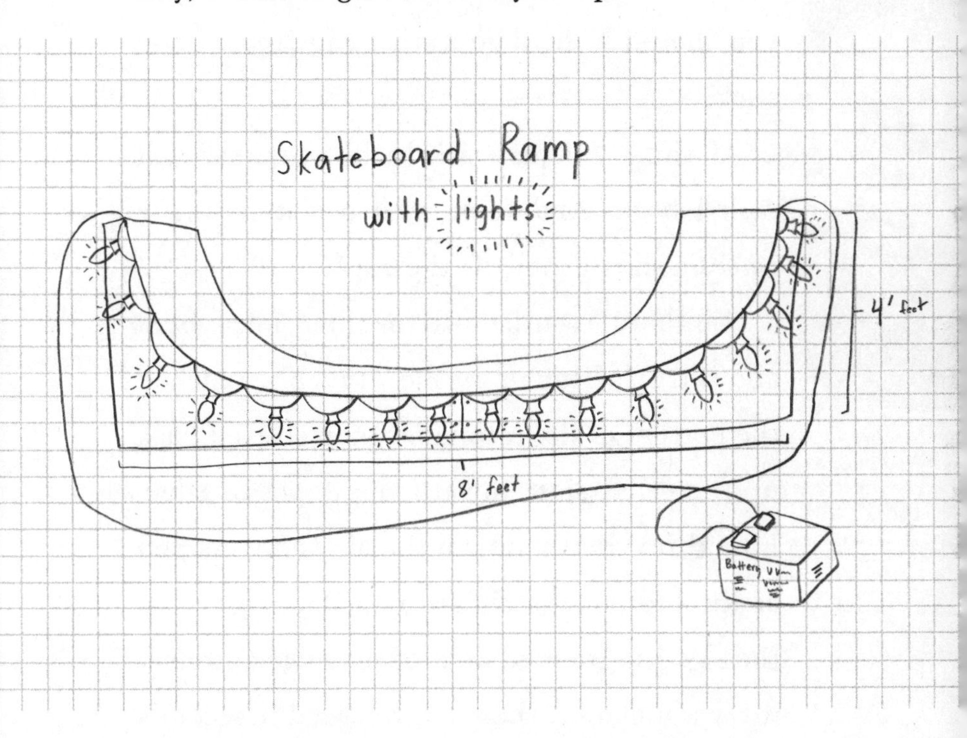

"If you fall, I know how to stabilize your leg until the ambulance arrives!" their friend Toby called from the far side of the driveway, looking very serious. Toby knew how to do all sorts of stuff like this, though sometimes it was more helpful than other times. He went on. "At least, I do if I can find a stick. Maybe you should wait to go until I can find a good stick?"

"I think I'll just risk it, but thanks!" Kit called back. And then with a clatter and a *whoosh*, she pushed off the edge!

Kit flew forward, down the ramp, knees bent and skirt fluffing up in the wind. She reached the bottom of the ramp and then started back up the other side, toward the opposite edge. Ellie threw her hands in the air and whooped as Kit and her skateboard launched right into the sky. Kit grabbed hold of the edge and held it for a moment, then she released it seconds before the skateboard hit the ground again with her feet planted right in the middle. Kit skated back down the far side of the ramp, back toward the middle, up, and–

"*Oof!*" Kit said as she pitched forward.

Ellie yelped.

Toby shouted, "I'll find a stick!"

But Kit knew how to fall off a skateboard—she'd done it plenty of times, after all, since that was how learning to skateboard worked. Kit tucked her arms in and rolled. In a split second, she was on her feet without a single scratch. The skateboard whizzed back and forth as it slowed down, then it finally stopped right in the middle of the ramp.

"Are you okay?" Ellie said, running up to Kit, even though she could already tell Kit was just fine.

"Yep!" Kit said cheerfully. "I think my wheels got caught on the lights," she added, then guided Ellie over to a spot near the top of the ramp. Her board had indeed gotten hung up on the string of lights and snapped it into two pieces. "Oh no! I broke them!" Kit realized, putting a hand to her mouth.

"It's all right," Ellie said. "You just broke the road."

"That doesn't sound all right," Kit answered, shaking her head.

"It is! See, look," Ellie said, and pointed at the place where the string of lights was snapped. "To make the lights turn on, the electricity has to go in a circle—that's why it's called an electrical *circuit*. *Cir*cle, *cir*cuit, get it? Anyway—you just smashed up part of the road, like the Godzilla monster did in that movie we weren't supposed to watch. All we have to do is fix the break in the road, and then the electricity can go round and round in the circuit again."

Kit didn't seem convinced.

"Watch," Ellie said, and took the broken ends of the string lights. She carefully twisted the bits of broken wire back together and *ta-da*, the lights blinked back on.

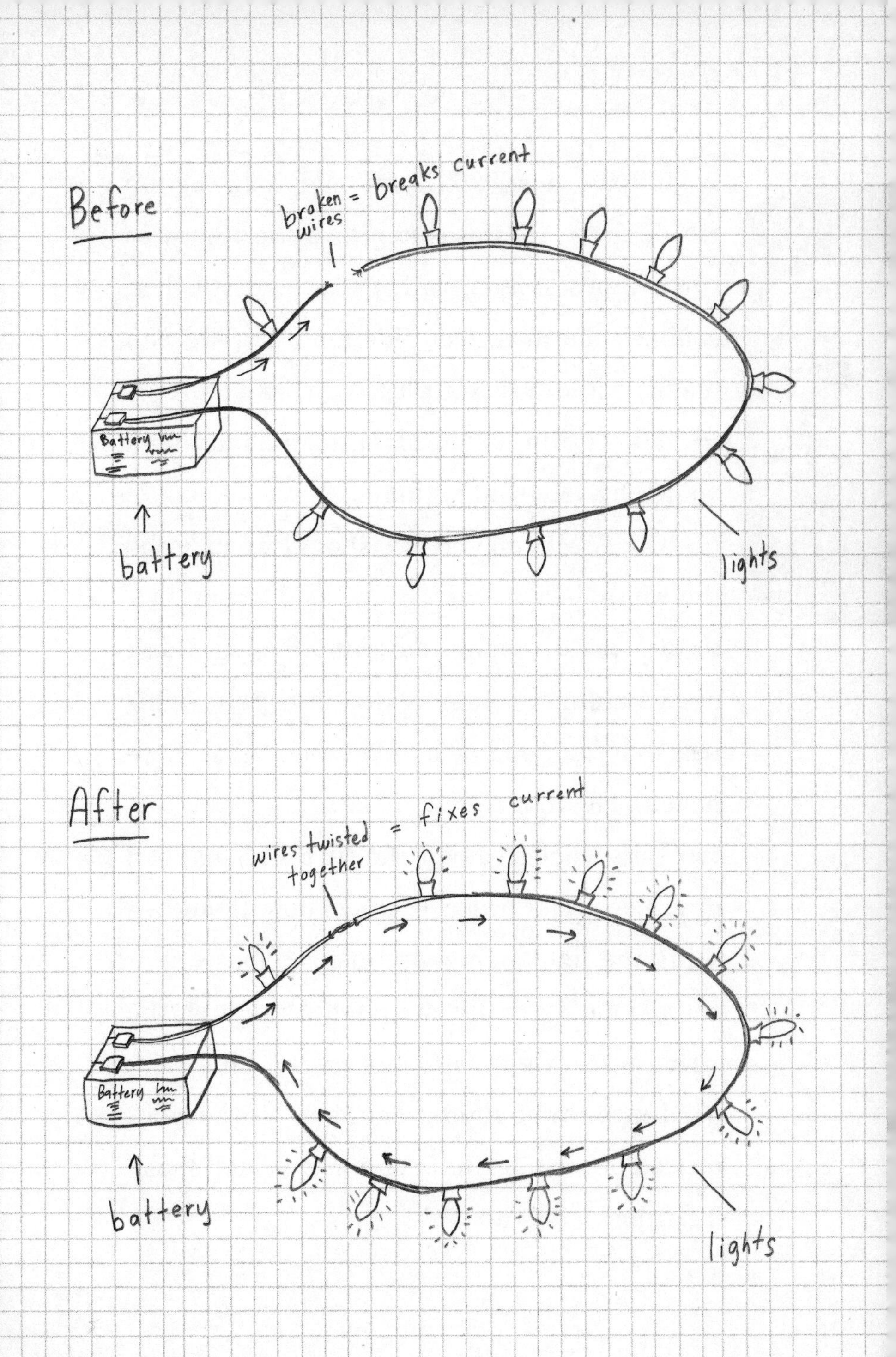
Before
broken wires
= breaks current
Battery
battery
lights
After
wires twisted together
= fixes current
Battery
battery
lights

"I have a stick!" Toby said, panting up beside them. He was clutching a stick that was three times as long as Kit's leg and still had a pine cone attached. "It's long, but we can maybe cut it to fit your leg."

"I don't think I'll need it after all, but thank you, Toby," Kit said politely.

"Oh. Well, maybe we should keep it by the ramp, just in case," Toby said, trying not to look *too* disappointed that Kit's leg didn't need stabilizing. Toby really liked putting his research to good use. "Anyway, what happened? The lights broke?"

"Kit's wheels caught the wire and snapped it, so the circuit broke. It's fixed now, though—I think the light string was just too loose, so it got all snarled easily—we ought to tighten the string up so there isn't any extra," Ellie said. "And maybe the lights should go on the sides instead of the top? But . . . hmm . . . that'll make it harder to fold up . . ."

Kit frowned. "If it doesn't fold up, it won't fit in my mom's car."

"Maybe I could put wheels on it, and we could *attach* it to your mom's car, and then we can *tow* it to the Miss Junior Peachy Clean Pageant!" Ellie said, eyes going big like capital "O's." It wouldn't be *that* hard to find wheels, would it? As long as Kit's mom drove very slowly—

"I thought it was the Miss Junior Pecan *Queen* Pageant," Toby said, interrupting her thinking.

"It's the Miss Peachy *Keen* Pageant," Kit corrected them both. "And that's a really good idea, Ellie, but I don't think my mom will let us attach anything to her car again. She made a rule about it, remember?"

"Oh. Right," Ellie said, frowning. Kit's mom made a lot of rules—there were the regular rules that most adults had, like the "inside voices" rule and the "no muddy shoes on the couch" rule, but then she also had a lot of rules that were made mostly for when Ellie was around, like the "butter is for bread not robot parts" rule and the "no jumping off anything higher than three feet no matter what sort of parachute / bungee cord / rope you have attached" rule. She'd made the "leave my car out of it" rule after Ellie and Kit had used her car to launch a kite into the air. Ellie thought it was pretty unfair, since the car had worked as a *great* kite launcher; it just turned out to not be such a great kite *flyer* when she drove under a stoplight, and the kite got caught and then fell onto the windshield, and Kit's mom thought it was a parrot attacking the car, and—

Well. It really wasn't all *that* bad in the end, but Kit's mom seemed to think it was.

"All right, let's think," Ellie said. "If we could put the lights on *after* we get to the pageant, that might work. But then they still have to get folded up to go to the stage, right? I wish they'd just let us put the lights together *on* the stage. That'd be best."

"Ooh, and if they *did* let you do that, that could be your talent, Ellie!" Toby said helpfully.

Ellie shook her head. "I just don't think that would be a good pageant talent."

Kit had begged Ellie to enter the Miss Peachy Keen pageant with her, and because Kit almost always did things that Ellie wanted, Ellie had agreed. Even better, Toby was going to come along with them, too. He wasn't going to be in the pageant, but his mom thought a weekend at a pretty hotel with Kit's and Ellie's moms would be fun.

The only catch was that this would be the very first time Ellie was *ever* going to be in a pageant, and she was pretty nervous. Fluffing her hair big and wearing lipstick didn't worry her—she liked lipstick, after all, and the way it left kissy marks when you kissed your arm or your electric drill or the wall—but the talent part had her feeling squiggly. Ellie knew what her best talent was—it was engineering!—but after doing a little research, Ellie had decided that engineering wasn't a good pageant talent. As best as Ellie could tell, pageant talents were supposed to be flashy and fancy and loud—like singing or dancing or, in Kit's case, skateboarding.

"Or maybe I can teach you to stabilize bones! If Kit breaks her leg, your talent will be *really* impressive," Toby said.

"I don't want to count on breaking my leg, though, Ellie, if you don't mind," Kit said.

"I don't think I have permission to break mine," Toby said with a shrug.

"It's okay. I'm just going to do my ballet routine," Ellie said. "But maybe you can teach me how to stabilize bones, Toby, just in case. You're right—that would be a really impressive talent."

"Yes!" Toby said, cheering.

"But before we start fixing bones—maybe I can try the ramp again? It'll get dark soon," Kit said. "I want it to be perfect for the pageant!"

Ellie gave her a thumbs-up. "Don't worry at all, Kit—the pageant people aren't going to know what hit them!"